An Irish
Girl

Also by Marilyn Hering:

A Woman Possessed

A Woman Beloved

A Woman Endures

An Irish
Girl

Marilyn Hering

AN IRISH GIRL

iUniverse books may be ordered through booksellers or by contacting:

iUniverse
1663 Liberty Drive
Bloomington, IN 47403
www.iuniverse.com
1-800-Authors (1-800-288-4677)

ISBN: 978-1-5320-1692-9 (sc)
ISBN: 978-1-5320-1693-6 (e)

Library of Congress Control Number: 2017901674

Print information available on the last page.

iUniverse rev. date: 02/06/2017

In memory of the millions
of men, women and children
who died in the Irish famine

T ara O'Brien stood in the doorway of her stone cottage with its thatched roof. She studied the beauty of the disk of sun against a background of bright blue sky, a few clouds scudding across it and the sacredness of the green swath of grass across their land. It was a gift for usually the weather was overcast and gloomy. She smiled at Tessie her Pig who was drinking at his trough, at Deborah, Danny, Dooley and Donahue, her sheep, lying lazily in the grass, at Bessie and Tessie, their cows munching on the grass. She could hear the neigh of Chestnut and Spotty in the barn. She looked to the right at the meager garden of vegetables of cabbage, wheat, and barley they were growing. The soil of Ireland was terrible for producing vegetables but it was perfect for one crop. Potatoes. She walked over to the field where hundreds upon hundreds of potatoes grew, their green, shiny leaves beginning to burst above the ground, bent down and pulled one from the ground. It was the size of a fist. She shook the loamy soil from it and could see it was a lovely color of beige, strong and healthy. She smiled. Potatoes were the main crop of the Irish; they averaged eating five to eight pounds a day.

She felt the strong hand of her father on her shoulder. "Ready for another day, Tara?"

"I am, da."

By the time they got the tools they needed, gloves, spades, pitchforks, wheel barrows, her brother, Patrick, freckle-faced with uncombed sandy hair, still sleepy eyed, stood in the doorway. He rubbed his eyes.

"You don't look so good. Better tell your mother to make you some oatmeal."

Patrick turned and walked into the cottage. He looked back at Tara and could see she was far ahead of him, spade and pitchfork in her wheelbarrow, ready to search for her first full grown potato.

She plunged the pitchfork gently into the trench in the earth. The leaves of the potato showed through the compost and sand mixture they thrived in. She took great care with the pitchfork for bruises and cuts could develop into pitchfork rot. Exposure to light creates a bitter tasting build up of food chemicals that she knew from her father were poisonous. She immediately threw the large potato in the cart and covered it with a tarp.

After they kneeled, exhausted from hours of work, the larger potatoes they'd found had to dry out a few hours and be placed in a shaded place before storage. They put them in the shed where they stored them year after year. It was not only dark but possessed good ventilation with a temperature in the high thirties. Autumn would turn to winter as they sat in the root cellar ready to take the family through the year.

Kathleen O'Brien, her mother, auburn haired with green-gray eyes, creamy skin, and a slender figure, thought by many to be the prettiest woman in Montague, Ireland, covered with an apron and twirling the fried potatoes in her hand, flipped them one more time and let them simmer another minute from the turf they had cooked over in the kitchen.

"And so who's hungry?" she shouted, then coughed.

After a chorus of "I am" she called them inside and distributed their breakfast.

"And how does the potato crop look this year, Liam?"

"Wonderful. Just wonderful," he smiled, entering the door of the cottage. "A bunch coming up slowly but surely. Beauties that will surely see us through winter."

She made the sign of the Cross. "Thanks to our blessed Father in heaven."

Someone knocked at the cottage door and Sean McConnell, a short, stout balding fellow with stained teeth and a good friend of Liam's, entered, pushing his dark hair from his full face.

"Will we be goin' off to Mass now?"

He questioned the group but had his eyes on Tara. He'd had a crush on her since childhood. Now that she would soon be eighteen, he planned to ask for her hand in marriage, pretty certain her answer would be no. But that was his secret.

"You know better than to ask me that," Tara's father frowned. "You know I haven't stepped foot in the church for years."

"You're a wonderful example to the children," Kathleen sighed.

Kathleen O'Brien had been a student at St. Theresa's Academy in Killarney in her younger days. She was a beautiful girl, even then, with her auburn hair and green-gray eyes and the rest of the girls in the class thought she would 'fit in' with them beautifully. But that was not so, for she was painfully shy. When the other girls were playing tennis or on the softball team after school, she was in the library doing her homework or reading. She had no great dreams for her life. Her main goal was to marry a man who made a decent living and wanted children. When she graduated the Academy, she got a position as a seamstress and was content with that. Her sewing was excellent and she made dresses for many of the women of Montague and passed her knowledge onto Tara. Then she met Liam O'Brien at a dance given on St. Patrick's Day. He was a good-looking fellow, his dark hair graying on the sides with intense blue eyes and a neatly-trimmed beard; but when he told her he had a farm and a great amount of acreage for potatoes, plus sheep, cows, and pigs, her ears perked up. This was what she felt was her goal in life. She had never known love and what it is like to care for a man passionately and so she settled for Liam. Before you knew it, they had a son, Patrick, and she was happy enough. She had no idea that the great love of her life still awaited her and; Kathleen, being a devout Irish girl, would face great conflicts over that love. Yet, it was one of the most important events in her life and would give it meaning she never imagined could exist. She looked at Liam now, with his overgrown eyebrows, scrawny hair and hairs protruding from his nose and wondered what happened to that good looking man she had met years back.

The church, Our Lady of Sorrows, was filled to capacity, as usual. Father Boyle who had been priest there many years entered adorned in gold and red vestments. He was a tall, handsome man with high cheekbones, a sensual mouth, a neat beard and clear blue eyes that crinkled when he smiled. He began the service. "In the name of the Father, the Son and the Holy Ghost. I will go to the altar of God."

The server answered, "The God of my gladness and joy."

Father Boyle continued, "Do me justice, O God, and fight my fight. Against the deceitful and impious man rescue me."

Alas, already Tara's and Patrick's eyes were beginning to close, try as they might to keep them open, especially for their mother's sake. It wasn't until the Consecration of the Host that Kathleen noticed and slightly elbowed them in the ribs.

Father Boyle held the Communion wafer in his hand and began, "Who, the day before He suffered took bread into his holy and venerable hands, and having raised his eyes to the heavens to You, O God, His Almighty Father, giving thanks to you He blessed it, broke it, and gave it to his disciples, saying, "All of you take and eat of this for this is my body.

"In like manner when the supper was done, taking also this goodly chalice into His holy and venerable hand, again giving thanks to You, He blessed it and gave it to his disciples, saying, "All of you take and drink of this, FOR THIS IS THE CHALICE OF MY BLOOD OF THE NEW AND ETERNAL COVENANT, THE MYSTERY OF FAITH, WHICH SHALL BE SHED FOR YOU AND FOR MANY UNTO THE FORGIVENESS OF SINS.""

After further prayers and Father Boyle's taking of the Communion, a long line of parishioners kneeled at the altar to receive the wafer they believed was the Body of Christ.

Among them stood Kathleen, their mother; Tara, her daughter; and Patrick, her brother.

Mass ended rather quickly after that.

Father Boyle stood at the bottom of the church steps to greet his parishioners. He gave a special smile when he saw Kathleen and her children. His face darkened when he didn't see Liam.

"I pray for the day Liam comes to Sunday mass, Mrs. O'Brien."

'I wouldn't count on it, Father Boyle. But, then again, we all know the power of prayer."

"Do you think he's given up on the power of faith completely?"

"No. I wouldn't say that. But he's very involved in –political things—his love of Ireland is very deep, Father."

Tara chimed in. "I believe he thinks the church should be more supportive of the fight for Ireland's separation from the British more than it has. And I feel that same way." Her comment emerged more as a challenge than a plain statement.

"We do what we can, Tara, but above all Ireland and its freedom is in the hands of the Lord."

She placed her hands on her hips. "It's not our prayers alone that will free us. We have to fight for our independence as well, even if it means violence." Her mother clenched Tara's arm.

"Enough, Tara! Father, forgive Tara's outburst. She's a very strong-willed girl." Another family approached Father Boyle, and excusing himself he turned his attention to them but not without a last glance at Kathleen O'Brien and her children.

"Perhaps you'll change your mind about violence, Tara, but that is a topic for another time."

She wondered how much he really knew about Ireland's past, that in 1801 the Act of Union between Ireland and England was imposed. England and Ireland became one. With the economy of Ireland incorporated into England, the Parliament in Dublin became nonexistent and the Parliament at Westminster legislated for both countries from that time on.

At first glance the Parliament was overjoyed, felt they had everything to gain for finally the discrimination of the English against the industry of Ireland would end. Combining with English wealth Ireland would finally attain the money she desperately needed for moving forward and developing to the best of her capacity. The hundred Irish members, the Irish believed, who were to be located at Westminster, would finally give Ireland a voice in imperial affairs. And also an impression had been created that when the Union became the law, Catholic freedom would soon follow, with Catholics freed and finally guaranteed justice and the laws that had prevented Catholics from membership in Parliament or judges would be repealed.

The truth of the situation the Irish soon found was very different. The Union's primary goal was not to improve Ireland but to bring her into complete subjection to the British.

And so, as time passed, no joy resulted and a pall fell over the Irish.

When they arrived home, her father was standing by the hearth roasting potatoes for them as he usually did every Sunday, his way of apologizing to Kathleen for not attending Mass.

He placed a baked potato on Tara and Patrick's plate and two on Kathleen's.

"I've had my food already." He smiled at her.

She did not smile back and plunged her fork into the potato he'd placed on her plate. Suddenly, she began to cough, not the usual cough one makes to clear the throat but a heavy, husky cough that sounded as though it was filled with phlegm. She took out her handkerchief and spit into it.

Liam punched the table with a heavy blow.

"For God's sake, Kathleen! When will you be goin' to the doctor to get some medicine and find out what's causin' that terrible cough? If it's the doctor's cost, I can easily work a few extra hours down at the shipyard. They can always use an extra hand."

"I'll be all right."

They ate the rest of their food in silence.

After eating, Kathleen picked up her sewing basket. She was an expert seamstress and often sewed dresses for her and any other repair needed to their clothing or that of her friends. She taught Tara everything she knew about sewing and Tara's dream was to one day own a dress shop of her own. Now she began to realize more and more how desperately they were beginning to need more money, especially with her mother's illness, and for any other needs they had. She made up her mind then and there tomorrow she would go to the British section to the more elegant shops to look for work., inquiring if anyone needed a seamstress. If not, she would take whatever job she could get. Her mother must get to the doctor.

Belfast was located in the northern section of Ireland but Tara knew the wealthier class lived there and the women would be much more likely to want to adorn themselves with expensive gowns and dresses.

The next morning she rose early, mounted Chestnut, and was on her way from their home in Monagham, to near the British-controlled area of Belfast. There had been an enmity between the south and north for generations and she prayed she would be all right as her hands shook on Chestnut's reins. The trip was long, but the shops had not closed yet. She suddenly felt foolish looking for work when she knew there were hardly any jobs. She walked the streets an hour or so and saw no signs in any windows asking for help. She was just about ready to give up when she spotted an elegant-looking shop with an awning that said in gold lettering on its window—"Bradford's-Specializing in Couture Dresses." Her heart thumped after she read it. Then at the bottom right of the window she read, "No Irish or Colored need apply." She clutched the sample of cloth she had embroidered showing evidence of her ability, took a deep breath, and entered. What had she to lose? The walls were wallpapered in maroon and cream stripes. On one wall were shelves with bolts of fabric, silks and satins mostly in red, navy blue, lavender, green, cream—so many colors. On the other wall was a printer's box, each square holding a spool of colored thread. To her right she noticed a table with four or five books on it, filled with pattern designs. The centerpiece of the room was an oak desk embellished with designs of flowers and leaves. Next to the printer's box was a cutting table and a curtained doorway which she assumed was for clients to be fitted for their gowns or dresses. On the far side of the room were three beautiful gowns already finished, waiting for their clients to pick them up she supposed. And the fabrics! Cream-colored duchesse satin, bolts of jewel-toned satin, softer rolls of sheets of silver faille, powder pink organza and other bolts on the work table or bundled in labeled bins on the pattern table waiting to be sewn.

An older woman with crinkled skin and piles of curls bouncing up and down was sewing meticulously. She noticed the liver spots on her hands. She stood up as she turned to observe her. She squeezed her eyelids as she examined her from top to bottom.

"Where are you from?"

"Monaghan. My name's Tara O'Brien."

"Didn't you see the sign in the window? This shop deals with the richest and fussiest clientele. I would surely lose business if I hired you."

"But I could stay in the back and no one would know you'd hired someone Irish."

She plunged into her pocket and handed the woman samples of her work: couching stitches, grass seed stitches, oblique stitches. The woman raised her eye brows. Tara had scwn a flower on the sample, a combination of satin stitches for the flower and French knots for its center, perfectly sewn.

"Come closer," the woman frowned. "The dress you're wearing. The bodice embroidered with red roses. Did you create that?"

Tara blushed.

"Yes, I did."

"It's just the kind of perfection I'm looking for. But we must have one rule. You must always stay in back of the curtain."

"Of course!" Tara clapped her hands.

"You won't be sorry, Miss—Mrs.?"

"Rouche. Miss Rouche."

"Your hours will be from eight until six. And your salary will be five shillings."

Tara would have worked for nothing to get the experience of working in such an elegant shop, but she knew her salary would help towards her mother's doctor bill.

She smiled as she rode all the way home. A slight breeze was blowing and she could hear the sighing of the trees' leaves which reminded her of dark gray lace swaying below the silver sky, the stars shining in the heavens looking down with tired eyes at the peaceful earth.

Dinner had been finished and she knew her mother would be especially worried as it was now dark. The branches and leaves of the trees now seemed like black skeletons. The sun was down and a light mist hung in the air but she was not afraid. It looked as though the clouds would burst with rain and she hoped to be home soon before then. A stillness settled across the land and sky, more typical of Irish weather, but she was so filled with joy she felt fearless. Finally she reached home just before the first lightning crashed across the sky.

Her father was frowning when she entered.

"And where did you go today, lass?"

"I know you'll be mad at me but I went looking for work. It's time I put in my fair share to help out. And I got a job!"

"Doin' what may I ask?"

"I'm goin' to be a helper to a fancy seamstress in a dress shop."

Kathleen squeezed her hand.

"Why, that's wonderful. With jobs so scarce nowadays."

"In—Belfast."

Silence reigned. Belfast was in Northern Ireland and parts were governed by the British, their arch enemy.

Her father stood up, knocking over the chair. "I'll have no daughter of mine workin' for the dirty British scrum!"

"But I won't be seen. I'll be in the back all the time, da. And it's such a wonderful chance for me."

Katherine grasped his arm, led him back to his chair. "Liam, it's a wonderful chance for her. She'll not be involved in their politics. Please," she began to cry, "Give her her dream."

Tara knew one thing Liam could never tolerate was seeing his wife in tears.

A few minutes passed. Finally, he grumbled, "I suppose you could try it out." He pointed a finger at her, "And there's to be no political talk."

So, thanks mostly to her mother, it was decided she would work for Miss Rouche. When the time came to plant their precious potatoes again, she promised she would do her share, rising earlier in the morning to plant them.

All seemed settled. For now.

She was surprised at the size of the back room when she fully stepped into Miss Rouche's shop, which was so large. Tara loved every minute of her sewing for her, and as the months passed she even gave her a raise of an extra shilling.

One day Miss Rouche went next door fifteen minutes of so for a cup of tea. From the back room, Tara heard the door to the shop open and peeked through the curtain. She saw a handsome gentleman, his hair dark and slightly graying on its sides, neatly combed, prominent cheekbones and tanned, as though he had just returned from a mission somewhere or other. He wore black boots, navy blue pants, and a red jacket with gold braid and an insignia that signaled he was a British captain.

She froze.

"Is anyone here? I need to pick up a gown for my mother for tonight. Is anyone here?"

Tara remembered that under no circumstances was she to leave the back room behind the curtain but surely he must need the gown for tonight and know someone was in the shop.

She took a deep breath and emerged at the counter.

"May I be helpin' you?"

As he looked at her, he appeared stunned. He observed her long auburn hair, trailing down her back, her creamy skin, her emerald-gray eyes. He had been with many women in his time and was somewhat of a gigolo, but none compared to the beauty of this seamstress. Tara was confused as he stared at her. Was he deaf?

"May I be helpin' you, sir?" she asked again.

"I—errr-a gown." He handed her a paper. "For my mother."

She stared at the order slip he gave her.

"Ah, that is a beautiful gown. I worked many hours on it and enjoyed every minute."

She went behind the curtain and emerged with a satin gown, each French seam individually pressed flat and smooth, with a low neckline and mutton sleeves. The bodice was completely beaded with purple flower designs and the skirt, a dark green, was adorned with purple beaded flowers to match as well.

"That dress is a work of art," he said. "And you tell me you created it?"

She blushed.

"Yes, I did."

"I wonder—this is so sudden I know—but would you care to share dinner with me sometime?"

"I don't think so."

"If it's because you're Irish, that means nothing to me. The whole idea of separation of British and Irish makes no sense to me. We should all live happily together. But, nevertheless, I must uphold my rank."

"It would hurt me to my bones. I love Ireland, you see. More than anything in the world. It would be a betrayal. But I thank you with all my heart for askin'."

Just then the front door opened and Miss Rouche entered.

Her eyebrows raised. "Forgive me, Captain Litchfield. I had to step out for a few minutes. How do you like the gown?"

"It's gorgeous. My mother told me to tell you she would be stopping by for another fitting soon. You certainly outdid yourself on this gown," he said.

He winked at Tara.

"Why thank you so much," Miss Rouche said.

She wrapped the gown carefully and handed it to him.

"Thank you." He turned to Tara. "And, please, won't you think about what we discussed?"

"Perhaps I will."

And then he was gone.

"And what may I ask did you discuss," Miss Rouche, her usual busybody self, asked.

"Out of the clear blue sky he asked me if he might take me to dinner sometime."

Miss Rouche's curls quivered up and down.

"One of our richest families, owner of Carlyle Hill, asked you? Does he know you're Irish?"

"Yes, he does. I said 'no' of course."

"You foolish girl!" was her only reply.

Tara and her mother sat in Dr Beel's small office. It had taken all these months to save enough payment for them to see him. Kathleen's cough had grown much worse and Tara was grateful she, a stubborn woman, had finally consented to visit. The office was in Monaghan. It was the only one for miles and people sometimes had to make a day's journey to get there.

Dr. Beel a tall, wiry-looking man with small features and stooped shoulders, led her mother into his office.

He placed his stethoscope upon her chest in various places and asked her to cough, doing the same for her back.

"How long have you had this cough, Mrs. O'Brien?"

"About two years."

"Two years! And you're only coming to see me now?"

"If only the British/Irish question was settled, you'd see more people in doctors' offices. It's shameful. That's what it is."

"Would you cough, please."

She did as she was told.

He moved the stethoscope to the other side of her chest.

"Please cough again. And then would you remove your blouse."

She blushed.

"It's quite all right, I assure you."

She did as she was told and once again felt the chill of the instrument upon her back. He had her cough six times, moving it a few inches apart each time.

"You can put your blouse back on, Mrs. O'Brien. And then would you wait in the outer office?"

He went to the door and called Tara in as Kathleen sat down on his couch.

"I believe your mother has tuberculosis. But, thank the Lord, it's not the contagious kind. A doctor discovered there are two kinds, the type that is very contagious and the one that is not. Your mother has the latter. I am saying that based on the fact your family seems not to have contracted any of its symptoms. Am I right? But waiting two years, for heaven's sake, does not give her a good prognosis."

"Yes, we're all all right." Tara's eyes were filled with tears.

"I'd like to see her every two weeks to keep an eye on it. I'm afraid it can become extremely serious at the stage it's at."

Tara was never more grateful for her seamstress position to help pay for the expenses of their visits.

She crossed herself as they left the office. She believed her mother's fate was now in the hands of God.

The O'Briens, as did the Irish in general, became more and more disenchanted when the promises made by the British in the Act of Union never came to pass. As time went on, by 1844 hope of investment of England in Ireland became more and more a fantasy. The only result of Free Trade between the two countries was that England seemed to be using Ireland as a market for any leftovers of their goods. As was bound to happen, Irish industry fell apart. Each day Tara became more and more grateful for her job. She thought that wealthy British women would always want new gowns as the fashions constantly changed, and they would want to keep up with the times.

Ireland sought a repeal of the Act of Union and by 1843 the demand was no longer ignored by the British government. The Catholic peasant began to organize as well as the commercial class. Rather large amounts of money were being raised, mostly because of one man, Daniel O'Connell. The British government was thrown into panic and feared Civil War. In the autumn of 1843 O'Connell announced that a gigantic meeting, the largest ever held, would occur Sunday, October 8, on the fields of Clontarf near Dublin. The meeting was forbidden by the government and O'Connell was arrested. If it hadn't been for O'Connell's strong belief that "human blood is no cement for the temple of liberty" a massacre surely might have taken place, However, he told the people, which included the O'Briens, to return home. The charge against O'Connell argued that he was attempting to alter the Constitution by force. He was sent to prison but the verdict was reversed by the House of Lords and he was released. But he became a changed man and his health was broken.

No outbreak took place in 1844. But something more tragic and heartbreaking lay ahead for the Irish ...

1845

The potato crop of the Irish was rather unreliable, even as far back as the 1700s. But the faith and hope the Irish people always had in its re-emergence as a fine and healthy crop was never shaken. The lack of reliability of the potato was accepted by them, along with that of the weather.

In July of 1845 the potato crop seemed to be flourishing, although there had been weeks of gloom before when the weather was hot and dry. The low temperature that emerged even after chilling rains and fog did not worry them because as of the ending of July the potato crop was never before looking so large and at the same time so abundant Freeman's Journal reported.

Tara stood outside her small, stone cottage and thought soon now she would be working during the day as a seamstress and digging up the potatoes from their trenches. She was glad of it; few potatoes were left in the shed and the extra shillings she was making still paid for her mother's semi-weekly doctor bills. The doctor said she seemed to be worsening, but she did not tell her father and Patrick. What good would it do? They had enough of a burden to cope with day to day with chores on their land. As she walked over to Tessie, her pig, to hug her goodbye, she could smell a terrible stench. Had one of the animals died? She surveyed them, checked the barn, and all was fine. She walked across the grass of their piece of land, and it seemed the smell got worse as she neared the potato crop; yet, their leaves were green. This gave her hope. She bent down shakily, dug up one with her hand. It was rotten and the black mush from it seeped through her fingers. Her heart pounded faster.

She raised her head to the heavens.

"Dear Lord, no! Please. No! Please," she cried and made the sign of the cross.

She ran down adjacent to the trench and dug for another potato. As she scooped it up from the soil, the rot of it once again slipped through her fingers.

She ran to the house, awakened her father. Sleepy eyed, he said, "It's too early to get up yet."

"Da, the potatoes. They have the rot. The potatoes have the rot."

He jumped out of bed immediately.

She began to cry, wiped her eyes with the back of her soiled hand. Liam was dressed in no time, ran to the potato field, and examined the crop in ten or twelve places.

"Dear God, how will we live?" His face slumped.

Their main meal of eight to fourteen pounds of potatoes, depending upon the size of the family, had suddenly vanished. Their land allowance was so small they hardly had any room to grow anything else, plus the soil was so poor most crops did not survive. Except potatoes.

Disastrous reports began to grow as the farmers gathered together. They realized very quickly that it was time to be ready to prepare for a famine in Ireland. The Constabulary Reports were the most depressing ever. In Antrim, Armagh, Bantry, Clonakilty, Bandon, Kinsale, Kildare, Wicklow, Monaghan, Tyrone and many other counties the main words reported were, "potato rot."

The traditional Irish method was to keep potatoes in a large pit, a simple task, and the tubers were to some degree protected from frost and rain. But common sense was replaced by fear. One suggestion was for the baking of the diseased potatoes in their primitive Irish homes for eighteen to twenty two minutes at a temperature of 180 degrees. When the blackish rot with a foul smell oozed out, they claimed the potato could then be peeled. This was useless when tried. The potato disintegrated into a slimy, decaying mass. Six months provisions which fed the Irish peasant turned into a pile of rot.

Tara was so grateful to rise early in the morning, dress, hug Tessie her pig and ride to Miss Rouche's dress shop. The payment she received in shillings, sparse as it was, allowed her to buy three loaves of bread each Saturday, which they rationed for the week, and still had enough for her doctor's visits. Unfortunately, since so much of the Irish peasants' land was needed for growing potatoes and had been wiped out, she soon was allowed to buy only one loaf of bread for the week because of the need of others.

After a few months of such meager amounts of food, the trip to Miss Rouche's shop was beginning to wear on her as she lost weight.

A few months later, much to her surprise while she was sewing beads onto a gown she heard the voice of the officer she had sold the green and purple satin gown to enter the shop and speak to Miss Rouche.

"Hello, Miss Rouche. I'd like to pick up my mother's blue gown, if I may. And she said she'd be in for another fitting in a few weeks."

"Certainly, Captain Litchfield. I'll get it and wrap it for you."

"Where is the young lady who waited on me the last time?"

"Tara? Oh, she's in the back, beading a dress for another customer."

"I was wondering if I could speak with her."

"Speak with her? With Tara?" Miss Rouche began to tremble. "Believe me, Captain Litchfield, I had no idea she was Irish. I—"

"Oh, it's not that."

Tara emerged from behind the curtain and she could see the look of admiration in his eyes.

"Tara," he smiled. "A beautiful name for a beautiful girl."

"Hello, Captain Litchfield," she blushed.

Miss Rouche scampered behind the curtain at that point to get Mrs. Litchfield's gown.

"I—wanted to—ask you a question." His voice was slightly trembling. "Although I know the answer will be no."

"Why don't you ask it and see?"

"I wondered if you would—have dinner with me, perhaps next Saturday at, say, seven o'clock?"

She did not answer quickly. A Britisher asking her to dinner? What would her parents say? Then again, if she had a full meal that would last her at least two, maybe three days, and leave more food for her family. Plus, it would be nice not to have to hear the constant growling of her stomach as the family attempted to save on food, knowing the coming months would be hard ones.

"Yes. Yes, I would."

His mouth widened. When he finally composed himself, he said, "Well, I'm delighted. Just delighted."

She imagined his carriage stopping in front of her stone house, and her family seeing a Britisher emerging from it.

"I'll meet you here." He smiled. "You've made me a very happy man."

"There's only one thing. I—don't have any fancy dress to wear."

"I wouldn't care if you came in rags." And from the look on his face she could tell he meant it.

Miss Rouche entered with his mother's gown, wrapped tidily.

"I hope she enjoys it, captain," she smiled. "A lot of my hard work went into it." Once again he stole a wink at Tara.

"I can imagine the hours of hard work you put into it, Miss. Rouche." He took the package and said his goodbyes. Miss Rouche was all aflutter, her curls jingling as she sat at her desk.

"Imagine! Captain Litchfield asking you to dinner! Why, they're one of the wealthiest families in town. They own Carlyle Hill. I'm sure you've heard of it." Tara's eyes widened, "Why, yes I have. I've often admired their beautiful gardens from afar."

"Promise me you'll tell me everything that happens at dinner!" Miss Rouche was more excited than Tara.

"And people are bound to ask about you. They'll know you work at my shop. What wonderful business that will generate for me, I'm sure. Just don't say you're Irish."

Saint Boniface Church was, as usual, very crowded that Friday night for confessions of the parishoners to be heard and hope for forgiveness from Father Boyle who they believed was God's representative here on earth.

When Tara's turn came, she entered the dark confessional box, the only light emanating from the seat where Father Boyle sat. He opened the slat that let light fall upon her, indicating he was ready to hear her confession. She suddenly realized she was trembling.

"Bless me, father, for I have sinned. It has been two weeks since my last confession."

"And what sins do you wish to confess, my child?"

He had immediately recognized Tara's voice. But they both knew that whatever she told him in the confessional would never be known to any other human being.

"I'm going to dinner with—a—British—officer. I feel I'm betraying my greatest love, Ireland, by doing this." She broke down in tears. "But, father, since the potato rot we've only eaten one piece of bread a day to conserve for the worse days ahead. We have hardly any money and don't know what will happen when the landlord comes to collect the rent. The money I do make goes to my mother's doctor. My father and brother go out and look for work. But there is none. My thought is if I stuff myself at this dinner I can do without a piece of bread for myself for at least three days and that would be more for them. But this man—he's British."

"Of course, you aren't committing a sin. First of all what you're doing for your family is a beautiful thing and the Lord, I know, blesses you for it. And hard as these times are and what you are doing, you must remember God loved the sinner, if you still think you have committed a sin. What I want you to do is pray for this Britisher so he sees the evil of his ways and gives us the freedom we deserve. That will be your penance.

Say a rosary for him. And what is this you say of your mother? Isn't she well?"

"She has tuberculosis, father, but not the type that spreads. It's getting worse and worse. My da and brother don't know, though now that she's laid up in bed, I'm sure they suspect it's something serious."

He did not speak for a time.

Finally he said, "I will pray for her every day. You have no real sins but say another rosary for your mother."

"I thank you, father."

Then he smiled. "And, my dear, accept as many dinners as you can get."

"Because of your permission, father, I will. I will."

He closed the confession box opening, and she sighed. She took out her rosary and went to the altar, praying for Captain Litchfield and then for her mother, feeling joy at having been absolved from the sins of the world.

Father Boyle sighed heavily for Tara did not know, most likely would never know, that she was his daughter

Saturday arrived. Though she hated lying to her mother and father, she told them she would be later that night because Miss Rouche needed her help on a rush order.

"Then I'll come for you, say around eight. I don't like you riding home in the dark," her father said.

"No. It's all right. I'm not afraid. And I'm sure it won't be that long." She was sorry her parents would be worrying about her for she knew she would probably be longer than expected. But she had no choice.

Her mother smirked. "I hope she's planning to give you some extra pay for it." She began to cough, much more heavily than usual. Tara was glad she would be paid today so that she would have the money to take her mother to the doctor next week, although, as usual, she would complain and say they could use the money for other needs.

Saturday night arrived and she rode Chestnut to LaVie Restaurant and tied him up in the back of the restaurant. As she stood waiting in front, she could not help but notice its impressive outside. Two large, tall, beautifully trimmed bushes graced each side of the door. The name of the restaurant was painted in gold gilt and the restaurant held a glass plating with the menu printed on it in gold lettering. She guessed the building must have been made of sandstone and it was painted in dark blue, which enhanced its gold lettering. As she stood waiting in front, a carriage pulled up and Captain

Litchfield descended. He looked so debonair in his black, knee-high boots, navy blue pants, and red jacket adorned with gold braid. He beamed approvingly at her.

"You look lovely."

"I'm afraid my dress is a little big. I've lost some weight."

"I think you look just fine."

When they entered the door, which was held open for her by the doorman, Tara was transfixed by the sparkling chandelier in the center of the room's ceiling which reminded her of hundreds of diamonds. She noticed the wallpaper was a maroon and white stripe with a hand-painted border of flowers—roses, daffodils, hyacinths, marigolds,—so many others surrounding the room. She observed each table was adorned with a pitcher of fresh flowers and the dining plates and rest of the dinnerware was trimmed in gold. She could not understand why each place setting was surrounded on three sides by a total of five pieces of silverware. She would have to watch and see what Captain Litchfield used.

Every eye in the room watched her as she was guided to her seat by the waiter. Who was this beautiful girl in such a somewhat dowdy dress? She certainly wasn't a local girl and must be from the surrounding area. Daughters of the mothers and fathers who were there looked quite despondent. Captain Litchfield was so handsome and a great catch, since his mother and father, Countess and Count Litchfield, owned Carlyle Hill.

The waiter handed them a menu, rather large and gold trimmed.

"I must say the food here is excellent," Litchfield smiled.

She had no idea what to choose and some of the dishes looked like they were in a foreign language.

'Why don't you choose for me?"

"Well, what do you like?"

"I love fish. It's so terrible how they kill animals and actually eat them."

He ordered salmon Lyonaise for her and the same for himself, feeling it would make her feel more comfortable.

He thanked the powers that be he hadn't ordered steak, lamb, or pork!

"Won't you tell me more about yourself?"

"Well, there isn't much to tell. You know I work for Miss Rouche. And I love flowers and animals."

"I noticed the beautiful red roses embroidered across the neckline of your dress. Did you embroider them?"

"I did," she blushed. "Red roses are my favorite flower. Someday I'm going to have a garden just filled with them."

"I don't doubt it. You seem like the kind of girl who, when she puts her mind to it, succeeds."

"And of course I have my pets—Tessie, my pig; Deborah, Danny, Dooley and Donahue, my sheep. Donahue is pregnant so we'll be birthing a lamb soon. It's so exciting." She clasped her hands together in glee. "And there's Bessie and Tessie, our cows."

"And, of course, we have two horses, Spotty and Chestnut, who's my horse."

"And how have you been faring with—the famine?"

"We're holding on. I'm so grateful for my job. It allows me to buy a loaf of bread each week and each day we have a piece."

"Good Lord! Is that all you eat? No wonder you look so thin."

"Well, we need to use the rest for my mother's doctor. She isn't well at all. She has tuberculosis. But don't be afraid. It's not the contagious kind. I also have a father and brother who've been searching for work for weeks. But there's nothing. And what about you?"

He realized this was not the time to delve into his childhood upbringing and background.

"Oh, I've been in the Guards five years. Last year I was made a captain. And I've traveled and been stationed in many places—Tunisia, Egypt, Arabia, France."

She brought her hand to her chest.

"You should be very proud of that. I doubt I'll see any of those places. But it's too bad you're British."

"Let's not talk about political things. It will ruin our evening, I'm sure. But I must say I'm quite disturbed by the famine and what's it's doing to the Irish people. It's heartbreaking. I want to see these terrible conflicts resolved. Why can't we all live together in peace? I sound like an idealist I suppose."

She looked upon his face and saw genuine sorrow upon it. She realized immediately this man was not the typical Britisher.

Dinner was served. She plunged into the salmon with her fingers she was so hungry. The string beans and baked potato that came with it were eaten in no time. She saw the supercilious glances of people around her as she chewed the food but did not care. Captain Litchfield was eating his that way when he saw her doing it, so it must be correct.

For dessert they had a caramel pudding with a dollop of whipped cream on it. She noticed he picked up a spoon to eat it, and so she did too.

They talked for quite a time. He told her about where his mother and father were born, about his childhood but steered away from any indication of his wealth.

When the check arrived, she saw it was twenty pounds; he paid quickly and left a generous tip. She had never seen that much money in her life.

"I've had such a wonderful time being with you," he said.

She did not respond as he hoped she might.

"Thank you so much for the dinner. Now I won't have to eat for at least three days and that food can go to my family."

"You have a beautiful heart."

His eyes looked misty.

He walked her to the back of the restaurant to Chestnut and helped her mount him. He kissed her hand and she could feel the passion sinking through him as he did.

She rode home carefully on Chestnut, the leaves of the trees ink blots against a dark gray sky. She looked up at the stars and experienced such contentment for she felt nothing, except gratitude for the wonderful evening she had. If only Captain Litchfield were not British, in time she might have cared for him. He treated her like a lady and she certainly was not used to that.

The following Saturday morning, with fear within her, she brought her mother to the doctor. The room they finally entered was white and sterile with a large white cabinet in the corner holding a stethoscope and various other instruments. Kathleen sat down on the edge of the cold examining table.

"Good morning, Kathleen." Doctor Beel smiled at her. He noticed a pale coloring upon her face which he had not observed the last time they met.

"Will you please remove your blouse so I can check your lungs with my stethoscope?"

She did so and he moved the stethoscope to her chest in six different places. Then he did the same as he examined her back.

"You can put your blouse on now. As you can probably guess by the probable progress of your cough, your condition is worsening. Ideally you should be placed in hospital but we know that you'd never agree to that. Am I right?"

"Yes. We could never afford it."

"So I'm ordering you to go home, take to your bed, and stay there." He glanced at Tara. Then he went to the cabinet and produced a medicine. "Take this every five hours without fail."

Kathleen wrenched her hands.

"But I can't be bedridden. There's too much I have to do. I—"

"She'll do as you say, doctor. Believe me." Tara interrupted.

"Kathleen, would you get dressed and wait for me in the outer office? I'd like to talk to Tara."

After she left and closed the door, he turned to Tara. "I'm afraid your mother's situation is very grave. I'd give her a few weeks or so and then you will find blood in her sputum. After after that let us hope she'll last a month more, if we're lucky."

"Dear God! That soon?"

"I'm afraid so." He placed his arm upon her shoulder.

"The fact that she's eaten so little with the famine doesn't help either. Though not contagious, this type of tuberculosis usually has a good prognosis, but the fact that she's waited months upon months to come see me is working against her."

'You know how stubborn she can be about doctors, about doing anything for herself."

"I certainly do."

"Please, doctor, don't tell my father or my brother the length of her illness. They couldn't bear it. I'll know what to tell them when the time comes. I think it's because she still insists on doing so much, even with this awful cough, that it progressed faster. She hasn't slowed down a bit. But, believe me, she will now."

Tara and her mother walked home in silence. The breeze fell softly upon them, the trees moving their leaves so soothingly in a myriad of colors. A scarlet cardinal flew past them. Her mother pointed at it and smiled, then observed the daffodils growing here and there with their faces bathing in the sun. And soon Tara knew her mother would never see this beauty again, never see her beloved Ireland again. She tried to regain her composure.

"The doctor said that your staying in bed and eating as much as possible is the key to your recovery. And faithfully taking your medicine, of course. That's what will give you strength—and hope you'll recover."

Her mother smiled at her.

"Yes, I'm very hopeful."

She did not notice Tara's tear-filled eyes.

1846

1846 arrived, and another year of rotted potatoes. And famine. Yet, the beginning of hopefulness engulfed the Irish people. There was the establishment of a Relief Commission and food was brought into the country at long last. However, the Irish knew nothing of the strict limitation of that relief and thought the government was finally going to help them. They began to have confidence in the British and believed they would be issued free food.

Six months passed since the rot infested the potatoes, and in many areas people began to starve, eating anything they could,—food that stank, diseased potatoes that brought sickness and death to their pigs and cattle. In some areas they were eating food so putrid they had to leave the doors and windows of their homes open. Soon illness, including fever from eating diseased potatoes,; made the situation worse in every county. Then came dysentery and fever.

Boards of Guardian finally set up fever hospitals, but it was not a permanent measure. It expired in September of that year.

The potato famine also endangered the payment of rents; a large population of the Irish was to prove unprofitable to their landlords and they were eager to rid their property of tenants who could not pay the rent. People were officially called upon by British officers for collection of rents, and their houses were demolished. They watched in horror as their roofs were destroyed, their walls crushed to pieces. Women wept as they clung to their destroyed property, clinging to shattered doors. The British forcibly removed them, children screaming with fright, husbands standing dazed and helpless. That night they slept in the ruins. The next day the foundations of their houses were razed, and no neighbor who had been able to pay the rent was allowed to take them in.

It became common for the evicted to create what they called "a scalp." They dug a deep hole in the earth, approximately three to four feet deep and wide, its roof composed of sticks and pieces of turf, and in this burrow the family lived. The evicted, when discovered, were hunted out and punished.

Tara looked out the door of their cottage watching as the British soldiers on their steeds placed condemned notices on most of them. She knew soon they would be approaching theirs. They had barely managed to pay the rent last year, but, finally, this month they could not for she was using any extra money she received from working for Miss Rouche for extra food for her mother. She lay, wide eyed on the makeshift bed they had made for her near the warmth of the turf burning. Her father paced the floor helplessly; her brother, Patrick sat in a chair crying.

The sound of the loud thump on their door filled them with terror.

"Open the door! Rent is due!"

Her father opened the door.

"We don't have it."

He began to ready the notice of condemnation and preparing to place it on their door.

"No! Please!"

She ran toward the officer; she was desperate. Then she immediately recognized him. It was Captain Litchfield.

Their eyes met.

"I swear we'll have it next time," she pleaded.

She could see the look of passion on his face, though he tried to disguise it. He delved into his pockets and brought out two large piles of coins and placed them on the table.

"Consider your rent paid," was all he said. Then he turned and left.

They were dumbfounded, all except Tara. And she knew why.

The Irish decided they would no longer take the treatment they had received from the British. Frightening reports began to reach the various villages. Starting at the beginning of April there had been in Kerry, Galway and Killarney Irishmen starting to gather in groups of hundreds of men led by their new, emerging leader, John Connally. A ship carrying provisions was plundered on the Fergus River. At Mitcheltown, a mob of about a hundred women and children held up carts going to the Commissariat store, slashed open the meal bags and stole approximately two tons. Similar events took place in the western and southern half of Ireland as well as some districts in the east. The only thing taken was food. The Relief Committee of the Gentlemen of Cork announced that on a trial basis Indian corn would be on sale. The result was startling. A huge crowd gathered and there was an amazing rush for the meal. A riot almost took place after they ran out of it. The Relief Commissioners, terrified by the shock of such mass hunger and also fearing an attack upon the Commission itself would allow no further distribution. The Commission later estimated four million people would have to be given food during, May, June, and July before the new crop of potatoes, they assumed, was edible. This, of course, was an impossibility.

Although the situation of the famine haunted Tara every day and she was grateful to still be working for Miss Rouche, she continued to see Captain Litchfield who seemed to believe that perhaps in time Tara would grow to love him. The main daily concern she had on her mind was her mother's illness. This beautiful, blue-eyed, auburn-haired woman turned into a skeleton with eyes closed most of the time, her lovely auburn hair now a dull lusterless gray. Patrick, Liam and she took turns sitting by her cot, now aware with the large gobs of blood that emanated from her each time she coughed that the end was near. Her mother could no longer speak. Tara also worried about her father who seemed in a daze. She turned to Patrick,

"Get Father Boyle. Quickly. And tell him to bring what he needs for Extreme Unction."

They soon heard footsteps. Father Boyle, red-eyed, rushed through the door, Patrick soon after. He carried a small, maroon velvet box which contained the objects needed for Extreme Unction, the last Sacrament of the Catholic church. He opened the box and placed it on the small table next to Elizabeth's cot. He could see she was barely breathing. He also took out two candlesticks, two wax candles, fresh water, and a wafer of bread. He wet his thumb with the holy oil from a jar in its container, then he motioned to Tara to lift Elizabeth's blanket and drape it over the front of the cot. He anointed her feet, each time emblazoning the sign of the cross into Elizabeth's flesh.

"By this anointing and his loving mercy may the Lord forgive you whatever wrong you have done by the use of your eyes, nostrils, hands ..." He touched those parts of her body as he spoke.

Tara sat on the bed, half heard him. The cold from her mother's frail hand rushed through her body.

Father Boyle placed the sacred wafer between her lips, "Body of Christ," he said.

He saw that Elizabeth's pulse had dwindled, then ceased.

"She has passed on," Father Boyle said. And then he stood up, eyes tear stained, closed the maroon box, and left. He seemed to find remaining there unbearable.

There was no consolation for Tara, Liam and Patrick. Liam lay across her body and wept. Patrick and Tara held each other with tear-stained eyes.

The news spread quickly of her death but they did not have enough wood to make her a proper coffin since so much had been sold for money to buy food. Patrick and Liam dug a gravesite for her within twenty feet of their stone cottage. One of the women, Mrs. Kristina Duffy, from the village, arrived soon and began the ritual of "keening," a wailing for the person who had died, common to the Irish beliefs upon the death of someone in an Irish family. She writhed and screamed until she lay on the floor, exhausted. The day of the supposed burial Liam, Tara, and Patrick still sat by her side trying to decide what to do next.

"She'll not be put in the earth without a proper coffin, not my Kathleen. I'll have no worms eat at by beloved," Liam wept.

The next day they looked out the window shocked at what they saw. The men of the village each carried a leftover board they had not sold, some small planks of wood, others larger and began to build a coffin. When it was finished, they moved it closer to the burial site. It was a crude coffin, but certainly it would do.

After it was completed, they placed it near the opening that had been dug in the ground.

Tara and Patrick approached their father.

"You have to let her go now, da. Remember, she's with God now. And the angels."

Liam stared at Kathleen's body with a glazed look in his eyes.

Patrick said, "Let me help you, da," as he grabbed his father's arm.

Liam, Patrick and a few of the other men placed her lovingly in the coffin and closed its lid.

Finally one of Liam's friends hammered it down with nails that sounded as loud as thunder. Father Boyle, red-eyed, stood with the group as the coffin was laid in the ground. "May I say a brief prayer for her, Liam? I think she would want it."

Liam nodded.

He opened his prayer book, his hands trembling, and read excerpts from the Mass for the Dead.

"O Lord, Jesus Christ, King of glory, deliver the souls of all the faithful departed from the pains of hell; that they fall not into darkness but let the holy standard bearer Michael bring them into that holy light which You promised of old to Abraham and his seed. We offer you, O Lord, sacrifices and prayers of praise. Receive them in behalf of Kathleen O'Brien whose soul we commemorate today. Grant her, O Lord, to pass from death to that life you promised."

Father Boyle knew Kathleen would have wanted to have a complete Mass said for her, but under the circumstances of Liam's watchful eye he was glad he was even able to say the prayer he did.

Suddenly there arose from the crowd a woman singing. It was Mrs. Duffy, a freckle-faced woman, obese, with hair the color of carrots and eyes as green as grass, Kathleen's best friend for years, who had performed the "keening." Then more and more voices joined in, their tear-stained faces singing notes that surely reached heaven.

> I'll Take You Home Again Kathleen
> Across the ocean wild and wide
> To where your heart has ever been
> Since first you were my bonny bride.
> The roses all have left your cheeks
> I watched them fade away and die,
> Your voice is sad whene'er you speak
> And tears bedim your loving eyes.

So I will take you back, Kathleen,

To where your heart will feel no pain

And when the fields are fresh and green

I'll take you to your home again, Kathleen.

Patrick, Liam and a few of his closest friends shoveled the soil upon Kathleen's coffin. Every shovel of the spades struck the voice of thunder as they thudded against her coffin, then scraped it with a hollow sound. Then they placed a marker of wood shaped like a cross upon her grave.

Exhausted and weak from hunger, the group departed, a few to their cottages which they could still pay rent for and many to the 'scalps' they had built for shelter, unable to pay their rent.

A quiet excitement and low whispers filled the air of Monaghan. John McGuire, who seemed to have taken the place of their beloved leader, Connolly, who wasn't well, was coming to their county to speak. In their wildest imagination most of the residents never expected this great leader and fighter for justice for the Irish to come here.

When Saturday night came, the church was overflowing with many men and women standing in its aisles and even the loft of the church to see this great man and what he had to say. They heard he had led raids on British ships docked in their seaports in the North and stolen food the British planned to sell in their own country and others for profit while the Irish starved.

He arrived on a chestnut stallion and on each side of him rode two armed men, his guards. He was a tall, strongly-built man, wearing a plaid flannel shirt, common khaki pants and boots up to his knees. His face showed strength as well; his cheekbones gave his face the appearance of strength, his defiant blue eyes emanated the character of a powerful man, his fleshy lips were pressed tightly together as he rode, his longer brown hair hanging three or so inches below his collar.

Tara, Patrick and her father watched him dismount and then from inside the church as he strode toward the altar area with a sure and steady stride. The roar of the audience was overwhelming as he and his bodyguards, hands on their guns and perusing the crowd, stood in front of the altar. He raised his arms to them and they slowly quieted down.

"Ladies and gentlemen," he began. "I'm calling upon you for help. We have discovered—and it's an undisputed truth—that large quantities of food are being exported to

England from Ireland during this terrible period of starvation of our people. Ireland is actually producing enough food, wool and flax to easily feed and clothe eighteen million people. Can you imagine?" He stepped forward.

"Yes, I said eighteen million people; yet, a sailing ship coming into one of our ports with a cargo of grain is sure to meet six British ships sailing out with a similar cargo. Ship after ship filled with wheat, oats, cotton, cattle, pigs, eggs, and butter blithely sails down the Shannon River, leaving Ireland, which is on the verge of starvation. The potato deluge has swept away all other food from our cottagers. As you know, the Irish farmer was compelled by economic need to sell whatever he managed to grow to pay the rent; and, of course, paying it is the first necessity of life. Many to most of you are now living in 'shales' having been evicted from your homes, unable to pay the rent. You've been forced, I know, due to economic need to feel resentment—rightly so, when food left in market towns under your own eyes is protected by a military escort of great strength." He stepped forward further.

"I have learned that instead of leaving the port at Belfast, which we have raided successfully three times, they have changed their tactics and are presently in the bay near Dundale. My men plan to attack it next week at a time I will tell any of you who volunteer to help us. They believe the Irish are stupid and lacking in knowledge of their change of plan. The men I already have who have volunteered, twenty, will get to its hold and carry away approximately forty pounds of meal they plan to ship to England. Anyone else who feels strong enough to help us and make that journey, please stay; and we will outline our plan. The only problem we still have is how to divert the captain. While the ship's men will surely be asleep when we raid the ship, the captain will most likely not be."

Tara stood up.

"I'll volunteer for that."

McGuire turned to her. He beheld a beautiful woman with green-gray eyes, flawless skin and auburn hair that fell down her back.

For a moment he was taken aback, then composed himself. "It's—impossible—for a woman to be involved."

"And why not? A woman is just the kind of diversion the captain would need, having been at sea, and very lonely most likely."

A look of surprise crossed McGuire face. The crowd began to murmur.

"Do you mean you'd even be willing to—." He did not finish the sentence.

"For Ireland, yes, I would. To help feed the starving Irish, to get them food, I would do anything. Yes. Anything."

The crowd roared with applause.

O'Rourke still looked confused.

"I don't know what to say."

"Say yes."

He paused a few moments, finally spoke.

"Yes." he said.

"Those of you who feel too weak to make the journey, please leave now. And certainly it's no shame on you. Those left will meet next Monday morning at l a.m"

Most of them knew they were so weak from hunger they would be unable to help.

After they left, to those who stayed McGuire outlined his plan regarding their meeting next Monday at one a.m., taking their rowboats and then stealthily removing their shoes. Each would remove twenty pound bags of meal from the hold and when they return distribute two cups of meal to each of the Irish in their district.

"This young lady," he gestured to Tara, "is the key," he said, "since all the men will be asleep and we can enter the hold where the food is stored. All except the captain who will surely be in his quarters at the upper front deck of the ship. She must arrive ten minutes sooner and gain access to the captain in his cabin and somehow keep him there."

"I have no idea what you'll be running into," McGuire said. "He may be younger but most likely older if he's risen to the ranks of captain. He may be smart as a whip and know something's wrong. In either case, I'm sure he'll be seduced by your charms."

"I'll be ready for whatever I encounter," she said firmly.

He asked if there were any questions, said he had picked that particular time because only a quarter moon would be shining.

After the men went on their way, he and his bodyguards mounted their horses to leave. It was then he saw Tara walking to the back of the church. "You don't mean you walked to get here," he frowned. "It's dark now."

"No, I came on my horse, Chestnut. But I would have walked if I had to."

"Let me follow you home. It can be dangerous out here with all the starving Irish roaming around." He gestured to his bodyguards to leave them.

It was the first time in her life she regretted having Chestnut with her.

She mounted him, she introduced herself, and McGuire rode at her side. A sudden warmth entered her at the thought she would be riding so close to him. He helped her get on her stallion while his men waited. She felt an overwhelming sense of passion seep through her, one she had never known before. She blushed as his strong hands helped her onto Chestnut. She glanced at him and could tell he felt it too.

"It's straight down the road until Carmkmaris, then left and straight to my stone cottage. I'm one of the lucky one with a cottage to go to, but that should be ending soon."

"And why is that?"

"I work as a seamstress and it pays the rent, thank the Lord. And I don't think it will end. The rich always have money for new clothes. But you never know."

"I've learned something. I didn't know there was a dress shop like that in Ireland."

She did not answer.

They finally arrived at her cottage. He helped her off of Chestnut and that same strange feeling of passion surged through her.

"I've got mixed feelings about you being a part of this, but if you're sure—"

"I am."

"All right then. Arrive ten minutes before the others."

"I will."

He was still holding her around the waist. She could see he was as aroused as she was.

"I'll see you then, on Monday," his voice was low and somewhat shaken.

"I'll—I'll—be there," she stammered.

The next Monday at ten to one Tara arrived at the ship "Pride of Britain." She had walked the rather long distance, fearing the sound of her horse's hooves might awaken the men on the ship. Miss Rouche let her wear one of the more elaborate dresses in the shop, thinking she was going to dinner with Captain Litchfield. It was a lovely cream satin embroidered at its bodice with tiny pearls and at its bottom there were embroidered birds around it.

She saw McGuire almost immediately.

"You look beautiful," he said as he studied her lovely face and green-gray eyes.

She smiled.

"I thank you," she blushed, "especially coming from you. But I must admit, it's part of my plan."

She removed her shoes, which had once been her mother's dress shoes, and carefully climbed the ladder to the main deck. She knew on every ship the captain's quarters were at the top front deck of the ship. She knocked on the door that said "Captain" lightly.

A gruff voice said, "Enter."

She did and began looking around.

She quickly observed stylish furniture, decorative features and well-made hardware. There was tongue-and-groove paneling, a window, and a china cupboard to show the opulence, she supposed, of the captain's quarters. The cupboard had cut-out shelves, possessing a set of beautiful flow blue china, illustrating how every-day furniture could be accommodated to a ship. His mahogany desk gleamed as he sat there.

"Where is he," she yelled. "Where is that cheating husband of mine?"

He looked confused.

"Madam, I assure you. I'm the only person here."

She charged across the room, opened a door leading to the lavatory. She knew it would be empty.

She covered her mouth.

"I feel—I feel a fool," she said. "I thought my source who told me he was here with a woman as well as you and another woman was right, that she could not be wrong."

She finally had a chance to study him. She guessed he must be in his mid to late sixties. He had jug ears, his face was scarlet red and filled with broken blood vessels, the sign of years and years of alcohol consumption. She was glad of that.

A half bottle of whiskey sat on his desk. She squeezed her forehead. "I'm so ashamed. Do you think I could have a drink?" She could see the lid and the bottle of whiskey two thirds drunk sitting on his desk. Another good sign.

She rushed over to him as he lifted the bottle from his shaky hand and poured her a small drink. She could see he had already been drinking by the tiny amount of whiskey left in the lower rim of his glass. She grabbed the bottle and poured him a large drink to the rim of the glass.

"Whoa! That's a lot of whiskey."

"A strong man like you can take it, I'm sure," she smiled. "I like a man who is strong and can hold his liquor." She moved closer to him. They clicked glasses. "A man like you and not like my weak husband."

He gulped down five mouthsful of whiskey.

"Why don't we sit on the bed?"

He looked dumbfounded, as though in a daze.

They went to his bed and sat down.

"Would you like to kiss me and touch my breasts? I know I would like that."

He reached towards her.

"But finish your drink first. A strong man like you, why, you're the captain of this ship, of all those men."

He gulped down the rest of the large glass of whiskey, half shocked, half excited.

They went to the bed where he slept. She lay down. He laid down beside her. She opened the buttons on his uniform and rubbed his chest, could see he was beginning to have an erection. She kissed him passionately. She opened the buttons on her dress, her breasts tumbling out. He went to grasp them.

"Not yet," she said. "I like to have a man hold me in his arms and slowly feel him against me. It's more exciting that way."

She placed her arms around him, kissed his neck, could see the whiskey was beginning to do its job. Surely, she thought, the men must be in the hold, loading their rowboats by now. But she must make sure. She let him feel her breasts and placed her hand on his hard penis under his trousers. He was completely aroused. She rose, went to the desk where the whiskey bottle was, grasped it, and filled his glass again. "Did you know it's better the more you drink? Drink it all."

"N-no, I didn't."

She drank a mouthful, then handed the almost full glass to him. He drank it all down. God knows how much he'd had before that.

She let him touch and fondle her, waiting for the whiskey to do its job. Finally, his hands became limp, his erection declined, and his mouth suddenly opened wide, emanating a loud snore that reminded her of a caw a few minutes later. She did not move those few minutes, had to be certain he had lost consciousness and fallen asleep. Try as he might to keep his eyes open, they had finally closed and she knew he was in a deep sleep, snoring.

After five minutes or so she carefully released herself from his grasp. He moved. Her heart began to thump. But then he fell back asleep snoring again. She slipped off the bed, grasped her shoes, and tip toed from the room, She peeked out the porthole and could barely see the rowboats in the distance as they carried the precious food for the Irish.

At the bottom of the steps leading to the hold stood John McGuire.

"Are you all right?"

"Of course. Why are you still here?"

"I—wanted to be sure you were all right."

She climbed down the tiny stairs of the ship into the last rowboat laden with two large sacks of meal and McGuire jumped in.

"Did you—did you have to—"

"Thank the Lord, no. I got him dead drunk and he passed out."

"You're quite a woman, you know."

They entered his rowboat, finally landed on the shore, and he carried his meal to one of the men.

"Take this rowboat. And remember, I want two cups of this meal to as many Irish families as possible. I'll see you in the morning."

His men brought him his horse.

Tara began walking towards home.

"You mean you're going to walk all that way?" McGuire frowned. "I thought you had your horse hidden somewhere."

"I was afraid the sound of its hooves would be too noisy."

He dismounted, lifted her onto his horse. God, no. How could she be touching him again? She gave him the directions to her cottage. They rode in silence, both filled with sexual tension.

When they arrived he said, "Will I see you again?"

"Any time. Any place," she said unashamedly.

"I'll be in touch. I never know where I'll be next. Wherever I'm needed most."

"I'll wait to hear from you."

She felt her heart would pounce out of her chest and was somewhat frightened for she had never had this type of feeling before.

She heard a knocking on the door of their cottage early the next morning. It was Maureen O'Flanagan, her dearest friend, holding a pot in her hand. She had once been chubby cheeked and overweight but because of the famine now stood slim and pale.

"My aunt made some soup from nettles. It tastes awful but she says there's nourishment in it."

She handed the pot of soup to Tara.

"Come in. And thank you ever so much."

"I wanted to talk to you about something."

"Sit down. What is it? Your aunt isn't sick, is she? I hear some of the people in the other counties are falling sick with high fever. Thank the Lord it hasn't hit our village that I know of."

"It isn't that."

She appeared hesitant to speak, sat down, folded her hands on her lap.

"Tell me!"

"I've been thinkin' of goin' to America. They say it's wonderful there and I could start all over again. You could go too with your family. Of course, it's because they want to get rid of us with the famine and all the sickness startin'. We're no fools. But I've seen pictures in magazines of America and it looks like a wonderful place to live, according to the ads."

"Leave Ireland? Why, Ireland is my life's blood. I could never."

"Well, think about it. What future do we have here? Maybe you could open a dress shop if you saved enough in America. I saw a picture showing a street in America in a Gazette and it looks like a wonderful place to live. A really rich place. And the Doughertys have been so kind. They're goin' to take care of my aunt and I'll send back as much as I can to help them out."

"My dream is to open my own shop in Ireland some day. This suffering can't last forever."

"I'll miss you so much."

They hugged each other hard and their faces became tear stained.

"You'll tell me all about America and write all the time, won't you?"

"Of course I will."

Tara heard a Relief Commission was organized. Masses of the starving applied for employment. The applications were overwhelming and the people became more and more outraged to the point of rebellion. Soon riots became prevalent, mobs charging through towns, begging for work. The numbers who applied became tens of thousands. The situation became more and more impossible. The problem was that the potato, not money, was the basic way the value of labor was figured out. Farmers and landlords would give the laborers a cabin and a piece of potato ground. They would work off rent first and sometimes two meals on a working day. The laborers never saw that money because, above all, it was first payment for the rent. The major reward was the patch of potato ground but with the potatoes rotted, all seemed hopeless. In a monumental setback, the British declared relief was to be brought to a close. Also, no more meal was to be sent to the depot which had supplied a bit of relief for it was now practically empty of meal.

Some men, women and children were beginning to be unable to stand; others seemed half dead with emaciated faces, bodies, and staring eyes, a sign they were obviously in a state of advanced starvation.

The next year was all the Irish looked forward to when they believed the blight would be gone and the potato crop would be healthy and hearty. They had the idea that plenty always came after scarcity. The Irish people were always known to be innately joyful and optimistic. Hope was at its peak in every Irishman's heart. In May and June of the next year the weather was warm and the crop of early potatoes looked strong and plentiful. In the spring there had been surprisingly frozen, drenching rains but then the weather turned absolutely glorious.

Then, suddenly, reports of the new potato crop showed that, once again, disease was destroying them. In fact, it was more prevalent in this crop than the year before.

The British felt that the only way to stop the Irish from becoming constantly dependent on the British government was to bring their operations of aid to a close.

Some of the British government wanted to import food for the poor but the officials at the highest level strongly disagreed to their desire to bring their aid to a close.

No preparation, though, even if made on double the scale asked for, could have saved the Irish people from their fate. Before the depots closed and the public works shut down, which, the year before had minimally at least helped; they now could have saved the Irish people from their horrible fate. Once again, every potato in Ireland was lost. As one passed through the countryside, people sat on fences looking at their decayed potatoes, clenching their hands and wailing loudly against the blight that had made them without food. In a distance of eight hundred miles or so one could see the stalks which, ironically remained green but looking closer the leaves were rotted, scorched black and the potatoes mush.

Tara heard a horse's hooves approaching and then a knock on the door. As usual, her father sat on his cot, unaware of the world around him.

Patrick opened the door to a pimply-faced, poorly dressed young boy.

"Message for Tara O'Brien," he said, holding a sealed envelope in his hand.

"I'll take it."

"Sorry. It must only go to Tara O'Brien."

Tara stepped forward and took the envelope, hoping that finally it was a message from John McGuire. She thanked the messenger and went to the farthest side of the room to read it.

"Dear Miss O'Brien,

Although I felt you were perhaps hesitant to see me again, you seemed to enjoy the dinner we had a month ago, and I do hope it gave you extra nourishment during these terrible times.

I would be honored if you would join me again next Saturday night at seven or so at La Vie as we did the last time, in the back room. I will explain further when I see you. Please send this messenger back with your answer—either yes (I hope) or no and then destroy this note.

Yours faithfully,
Thomas Litchfield

She turned to the messenger.

"Tell him I said "yes.""

She was not foolish enough to turn down a delicious meal, no matter who offered it at this point of the stage of hunger she was in.

When she arrived, she was wearing a white dress she had made with satin fabric Miss Rouche had given her, red roses embroidered upon its bodice and around its hem. She had taken it in, but she still looked so thin, her cheeks sunken and her body somewhat emaciated.

"May I help you?"

The waiter looked her up and down superciliously as she stood in the doorway.

"I'm meeting Captain Thomas Litchfield here."

The waiter's eyes widened.

"Surely, madame."

He rushed her through the main dining room to the very back corner of the restaurant. Litchfield stood up when he saw her.

"My God! You look like a skeleton! But still beautiful..."

"I'm so grateful you asked me to dinner. As you can see, I've eaten very little lately."

"The situation hasn't been good."

"Just awful. My father seems to be more and more overwhelmed by the death of my mother and I can't do a thing about it. He just sits on our fence all day looking at the rotted potato crop. My brother, Patrick, is a godsend. Yesterday he found a bunch of nettles and three birds' nest eggs so with the piece of bread we divided we had a decent meal."

Litchfield put his hand to his face.

"You can't go on like this."

The waiter appeared with the gold menu.

"What do you suggest, Thomas?"

"Well, since you like fish the scallops, shrimp, and pollack in butter sauce are wonderful, with string beans and rice and for dessert peaches and ice cream."

"Yes, I'll have that. It sounds wonderful. Two portions of each."

"And I'll have the same." He cleared his throat. "But one portion only."

"Very good, sir."

After the waiter left, she noticed Litchfield's hands were shaking.

"Are you all right?"

"I—think I am." He smiled. "I—I—need to ask you something and I hesitate to do it. It's so impossible."

"Why, what is it? It can't be that impossible."

"I've—I've fallen in love with you. From the first time I saw you. If such a thing is possible. I've never felt so strongly about any other woman—and, alas, I hesitate to say, there have been many."

"I guessed that. After all, you're a very handsome man."

He blushed.

She hesitated a few moments before she spoke.

"Thomas, you've been so good to me. And I do think the dinners I've had with you have helped to save my life. I really mean it. They've given me extra strength—certainly more than that of the poor souls I see dead or dying along the road from starvation. But I have to admit I'm disgusted concerning what the British are doing exporting their goods to other countries so they can make a profit, letting the Irish starve."

"I know you're right. And every day I think of myself as being a coward for putting up with it. But—you still haven't answered my question."

She sighed.

"I think you know in your heart I could never truly love a Britisher, though I must say you are a very attractive man. I know you'll eventually find someone else to love."

"Never."

"And I think it best we don't see each other after tonight."

'But I have no qualms about buying you dinner. It makes me feel good to know I'm helping you."

"You see, I've fallen in love with someone else, Irish, of course; and I know he would be against it, even though I'm not even sure he loves me."

"I can guarantee he does. Or he's a fool. Who is it??"

"I can't say."

"'But you can still see me for food! I don't care. As long as I can see you, help you."

"That wouldn't be right. And I know he would never forgive me for seeing a Britisher."

"Will you ask him?"

"No, I don't think so."

"If he loves you, he'll say yes, if he truly wants your welfare."

They dined mostly in silence. When they parted, she kissed him on the cheek and walked away. A sense of hopeless grief overcame him as he walked to the barracks.

The next year, as the potato blight continued, the conflict between the English and the Irish worsened. English newspapers declared the Irish were certainly not famine victims but sneaky and bloodthirsty desperados. Cartoons were published every week depicting Irishmen as filthy, brutal people, assassins and murderers begging for money, making believe, under pretending for food they wanted to spend it for weapons; and with the contributions given to them from the British relief funds, they were buying arms.

Even though there was so much enmity against the Irish, when the potato crop failed once again a new relief fund was suggested. The British declared they would, once again, start a relief fund but they refused to pay half the cost. Half the expenses were to be paid by whatever district where the works were carried out, which, of course, for the destitute Irish, was an impossibility.

The British government also said they would no longer import or supply any food to the Irish. It would be sent abroad where they could make a profit from it. Only the west of Ireland would receive special treatment to the worst hit areas: Kerry, Donegal, the county west of the Shannon and the part of West Cork, including Skibbereen and the Dingle Peninsula, an area where the people lived only on the potato, where no other kind of food existed; there and only there British food depots would be set up.

When another failure of the potato crop occurred, more and more riots broke out. Panic seized Ireland. The people clung wildly to public works as their only hope to stay alive but British measures were utterly inadequate. Protests and violence suddenly became rare; the main feeling of the Irish people was one of total despair. Fear of famine lingered in their hearts and souls; they knew they were helpless.

Nothing was done; nothing could be done. Then an even worse situation took place. There became a general shortage of food in Europe. Not only was the food the British were sending to Europe for profit but also the expected imports from Europe were not arriving. The British government could hardly find any supplies to send to Europe at all. All over Europe the harvest of the later 40s was mostly a failure. The wheat crop there was minimal; oats and barley as well as rye and potatoes were a total loss. European countries outbid Britain for food which meant even less food for Ireland. But private enterprise was abundant. They offered food to Ireland at the highest price, meal, for example, except it was at unattainable cost. Dealers bought up whatever came to market and would offer it in small amounts at high prices the poor could not afford.

Patrick arose early, as usual, to see if he could snare any linnets or eggs they had hatched from a secret place he found in the density of the forest. It was not an easy task to snare them, but yesterday he caught two. Tara removed their feathers and cooked them over the minimal turf they had left. He also found one of their eggs. He sat by the stream a few hour before he saw the four of them flying up into the pine trees. He grasped the home made net he had made and as they swooped down he snared one. Now he must wait another hour most likely before, if he was lucky, he could snare the other one, then climb up the tree very carefully to search their nest to see if there were any eggs in it. He snared the second one and clasped the wooden cover he had fashioned over them. Then he climbed the tree and said "Hallelujah!" when he saw not only one but two eggs in the nest. He carefully put them in his pocket and climbed down the tree very slowly, placing them in their wooden-covered basket.

He heard a rustling in the trees but was not afraid. It was probably just the wind. But then he was taken aback when a giant of a man emerged with bare feet and torn clothes. His hair was scraggly and greasy, as was his beard. He could tell that at one time he was a strong, heavily-built fellow, but the main characteristic Patrick noticed was his yellowed teeth and frightening hollowed brown eyes, half closed, as he stood there weakly, his one hand on the tree to support him.

"What's that ya got there in the basket, boy?"

"Oh, nothing much."

He pushed Patrick to the ground, opened the basket, and grabbed one of the birds. He put it in his mouth and ate it, feathers and all. The bird's guts streamed down his chin.

"Please ... I have a family to feed."

"And so do I. That's the first I ate anything in days and days."

A sense of pity over came him. Plus he knew he had the birds' eggs in his pocket.

"Please. You can take the others. From the looks of you, you need to eat even more than I do."

"Ya mean yu'd let me have them? The way the times is?"

"Yes, I would."

"Well, God bless you, my lad," he said, stumbling through the woods, taking the basket.

Tara and Liam were disappointed there were no birds to cook, but they understood when Patrick told them his story.

"I'm proud of you," Tara said. "You did the right thing. Plus the eggs will be good enough nourishment."

British leaders, in spite of their experience in the past never came to understand the role of the grain harvest to the Irish. They only grew grain and oats to pay the rent, not to eat. It was well known that was their primary concern because failure to pay the rent meant they would be evicted from their cottages. They were given a bit of grass and were left to the mercy of the landlord. With the potato famine it became necessary for the renter to eat his growth of grain and oats; yet, he could not. This was the situation of Tara's family when she heard a British officer banging on the door for rent collection again.

He had said, "I'll take this cottage" to another recruit. "Take the one next door."

"Yes, sir," she heard the recruit say.

She opened the door and to her shock saw Thomas Litchfield, his index finger to his lips. "We're just supposed to supervise," he whispered.

Her father sat in his usual dazed state and Patrick was out trying to find birds and their eggs as well as nettles for the soup they hated but provided at least some nourishment.

"I had to see you. I don't suppose you thought about having dinner with me again."

"Truthfully, I'm torn between yes and no. I'm so hungry."

"But certainly not wanting to see me I take it."

"I didn't say that."

"I don't suppose you have the rent."

She began to shake.

"No."

He closed the door, held her in his arms. She was comforted by the warmth of him.

"I can't stay very long."

He delved into his right pants pocket and placed the money in it on the table, then did the same for the left one and the two in his jacket pockets. It was more than she would need for rent.

"Take it."

"But I can't pay you back."

"Of course you can. If you think about having dinner with me again. I somehow can't seem to let you go. And put the money in your pocket before my recruit knocks at the door."

Tara began to cry.

"I have so much to thank you for."

"And please remember there are no strings attached to what I give you." He paused.

"I'm giving it out of love. I pray that I'll hear from you soon. But, if not, I will try to understand."

The recruit banged on the door. Litchfield opened the door.

"They couldn't pay, sir. So I gave them an eviction notice."

"Let's go."

Litchfield looked back at her before he closed the door.

Some other feelings of humanity did occur, and some landlords reduced their rents or decided to forego them altogether. But that gesture was certainly not the norm.

Tara kept up her knowledge of John McGuire via newspapers. They reported that as food streamed out of the country serious riots were taking place all under the leadership of McGuire, more serious than any riots of the previous years. At Younghal, near Cork, a tiny port used mostly for export, a riot took place. A large crowd of Irish peasants tried to hold up a boat filled with export oats. Police were sent for and the group dispersed at Youghal bridge.

Another riot, with loss of life, occurred at Dungarvan, County Waterford. A large crowd of famished unemployed led by John McGuire threatened shopkeepers and merchants, ordering them not to export grain and destroyed their shops. Some of the plunderers were arrested and locked up. The First Royal Dragoons were called out. They were hit with large stones as a Dragoon read the Riot Act. The Irish would not listen, and a Dragoon gave the order to fire. Finally the crowd retreated but not before several men were injured and two dead. A large reward was placed by the British for McGuire who had not only led these riots but several others previously.

The public works started again but even if all food had been kept in the country, the Irish people would not have been able to buy it. They were penniless. Work was delayed due to the gigantic amount of applications that had to be sorted through.

When work did begin, immense problems occurred. All works were to be executed "by task" meaning payment was to be by results, in proportion to how much work was accomplished. The Irish hated "task work;" they felt stewards showed favoritism and the Board of Works was so short of employees it was impossible to get work measured properly enough for the correct payment they so desperately needed.

The payments allotted for an Irishman and his family were practically nothing. Also, the payment of wages was irregular. Then there occurred a shortage of silver coin which caused a serious delay in payment. It was finally decided that no works were to be undertaken where one person in the district would be paid more than the other. The drainage works which Ireland needed so desperately could not be touched since owners of lands bordering on a drainage area would have their property improved and increased in worth, while those who had property farther away would not benefit. This became true of every undertaking that was proposed, except for roadmaking. But that had been undertaken in previous famines. Ireland already possessed a great number of roads already; their roads were nearly perfect and they had plenty of them in good condition.

The situation grew more and more hopeless.

Then the next year after October 1 vegetables were finished growing and eaten. Normally, this became the time the Irish became dependent on the potato—and now with another blight the people began to starve for there were no potatoes at all. Food prices rose to such heights that finally the government decided to open a food store, but even the people who had been hired were starving. They could not pay such high prices. Finally, the Board of Works declared more depots should be open immediately in remote areas of the country, such as Inniskill in County Donegal which was at least forty-five miles away from the closest market. The Board of Works refused. The truth was the depots could not be opened because they did not have enough supplies and were almost empty.

Applications to the Relief Committee came in by the hundreds, the people saying their districts were starving and begged the British to open depots at fair prices. They did not realize there was a practical reason why the depots could not be open. They were almost empty. The government lied telling them there were large supplies that would arrive in January or December, which had no basis in fact.

Milling continued with great difficulty as well since the mills were always occupied by merchants milling grain mostly for export where they could get higher prices.

Unground Indian corn was available in some places. The main problem was it was sharp and irritating—it can even pierce the intestines and is impossible to digest. Even boiling it for an hour and a half did not soften the flint-hard grain, and when eaten produced agonizing pain, especially in the children. People in remote areas starved; the others continued to live on nettles and weeds, and, if especially fortunate, an egg or two from birds' nests now and then, or on boiled cabbage leaves as long as they lasted.

Upon receiving a note from Thomas Litchfield, a captain of the British guards, Tara was confused. She had told him she did not want to see him again. Then again she might find out what the British plans were regarding the Irish and McGuire. Plus, upon rethinking the situation she decided a dinner would be worth it and Father Boyle approved. She must see him face to face instead of writing a letter back. Come what may, she knew her heart and soul belonged to John McGuire who, ironically, she had no idea when, if ever, she would see again.

She took in her white dress she'd embroidered with red roses once again, somewhat embarrassed she was wearing the same dress and her mother's dress shoes.

As the waiter led her to their table at "La Vie" and as they sat down she studied Litchfield. He reminded her of the Greek gods she had seen in her picture books when she was a little girl. Surely he would find no trouble finding a woman with whom to share his life.

The waiter brought the menus and she could hear her stomach grumbling. She wondered if he heard it too.

"I see you have that lovely dress on. The one with the embroidered red roses. It suits you perfectly." He smiled, showing his perfect white teeth. "I'm so glad to see you."

"And I'm glad to see you too, I think."

He frowned.

"What does that mean?"

"I feel so guilty eating these wonderful dinners. Yet, I know they're what are keeping me in better health than almost any other Irishman I see. And I can share more food with my family because of it."

The waiter appeared with the menu.

"I know you like fish so I'd suggest scallops, shrimp and cod in butter sauce."

"I'll have a double portion of everything," she said.

"I'll have the same, only a single portion."

"Very good sir," the waiter said. Why did this woman always want double portions?

"I have a feeling he knows I'm Irish." She touched her arms, skinny and scrawny. "I can never thank you enough for these wonderful meals."

"There's something I need to tell you," he said, "so why don't I begin?" His face was flushed.

"All right."

"I'm—in love with you and want to marry you. I'm embarrassed to say it, but I've been with many women, and I haven't felt the way I do about you with any of them. Not even close."

"But you're British!"

"I've thought about that long and hard, and I' d be willing to leave the captaincy and the Guards themselves if you'll marry me. We could start over somewhere else."

"But—"

"Wherever you choose. Europe? Perhaps Australia? But I must have you as my wife. I can hardly sleep thinking about you, what you're doing, where you are. I—"

"Thomas, you must stop this. I'm in love with someone else. I hardly know him, as you do me, which makes it ridiculous, I know. But I do know what love is, what it feels like to feel love for another person."

"My God, no." He clutched his fingers to his forehead. "I thought perhaps it would pass."

He did not speak for a time.

He finally said, "Is it someone I know?"

"No, I don't think so. We've been through this discussion before. But please don't ask me any more question because I can't answer them."

"I-m astounded."

"I know I've hurt you so much and you've been so good to me. I'll have to live with the guilt of it for the rest of my life."

"You're foolish to say such a thing. You can't mean you won't see me again. You can't!"

"I'm afraid that's so. My mind is made up. It would be wrong because I'd be leading you on. I'm in love with someone else and that's that."

"How will I ever go on without looking forward to seeing you?" He rubbed his fingers through his hair.

"Thomas, a good and handsome man like you will find someone else, I know. Someone worthy of you."

"Never." He placed his head down.

"And you'll be so busy fighting the Irish."

"I shouldn't say this but all British ships will be guarded by one or two armed men from now on. You must be extra careful. And there will be more of a British presence in the towns as well."

Tara had learned an important piece of news.

They had their dinner.

"I think we should get the check," she said. "I've got quite a ride home."

"Can't you stay—a bit longer."

"I don't think that would be a good idea."

He paid the check, regained his composure.

When they arrived outside, she turned to him. He kissed her passionately. She pulled away and kissed him lovingly on the cheek.

"Goodbye, Thomas. And I'll never forget you and how good you've been to me in these terrible times."

"Goodbye, Tara. I'll never forget you. And I'll always love you."

He walked to the back of the restaurant with her and helped her mount her horse.

She disappeared into the distance and his life fell apart.

Thomas Litchfield knew he was a fortunate man in many ways. His family and Carlyle Hill went back almost a hundred years. His great grandfather, grandfather, and father had served in the British army; and, of course, it was expected he do the same, although his father hadn't the least suspicion, he was not happy as captain of the British guards. It had taken him five years to attain that rank. His father was a firm believer that he not receive any special treatment because of his background. But he managed to survive the post well enough. He had been to Egypt, Tunisia, Germany, France, and Saudi Arabia during his earlier years in the guards and was grateful for the experience. Yet, in his heart, he thought it all a sham. Why couldn't all people get along? Why did there always have to be war and conflict? And so his role, when he was finally appointed to Captain of the Guards was one he accepted with mixed emotion.

And then he met Tara. Here was a girl he was fighting against in a battle that to him was senseless. Her beautiful face haunted him—her green-gray eyes, her perfect skin, her auburn hair that flowed down her back, her delicate features and charming personality, and thought: this is supposed to be the enemy. His heart was split in various directions, whether to be true to the Guards or to leave them and side with the Irish which would absolutely break his father's heart. What the British were doing to the Irish was wrong, just damned wrong. And he was part of it. And he knew, as the vision of his background and especially of his father's face appearing before him and the remembrance of Tara's gaunt face and sunken cheeks, would haunt him until the day he died.

Famine in Ireland had finally gotten to the point where almost complete disorganization occurred. Groups of starving men, women and children roamed the countryside, begging for food. The unemployment lists became a farce, and fear of the local mobs began. Men constantly poured into the Relief Committee's office saying neither their lives nor their properties would be secure if they returned to their houses without promise of employment. Some forced themselves in, crowding the works in progress and insisting upon working, to no avail. Also, delays in paying wages increased. The pay clerks in East Carbury in County Cork gave up their precious jobs out of fear of the turbulent masses. In another county the pay clerk was attacked and beaten. A man named John O'Reilly died while working on road No.1 in County Cork. The post mortem exam showed his death to be the result of starvation. He had no food in his stomach or small intestines, except for an undigested portion of raw cabbage leaves.

Autumn was now passing into winter. The nettles, blackberries and edible roots and cabbage leaves hundreds had been living on disappeared. Groups of starving men, women, and children roamed the streets and nothing edible survived.

Children began to die. In Skibbereen in the work house fifty per cent of the children admitted starved to death.

At this time of suffering unbelievable weather added greater hardship to the people. Ireland is famous for its mild weather; sometimes years pass without any snow. In the gardens in the south and west even semi-tropical plants bloomed, and dahlias, which are tubers, can be left for the winter in the ground without any worry concerning frost. But this year of 1846 at the end of October it turned extremely cold and, unbelievably, it snowed in November, at least six inches.

Had God forgotten the Irish? What had they done to deserve such pain and suffering, for the winter of 1846-1847 was the most severe in living memory. Frost was continuous and icy gales blew sleet and hail with disastrous force. Since the climate was usually mild and a supply of peat or turf almost universal in the country, a turf fire usually burned in an Irish cottage night and day, normally not going out. Usually the Irish peasant spent the cold, winter days indoors; and even though he was dressed in rags and his children naked, they were able to see things through.

But this winter was a different story. He had to go out, drenched with rain, snow and icy gales and try to make some sort of meager living. These laborers began to faint from exhaustion. There were an increasing number of deaths at the works from starvation, aided by exposure to cold, snow, and drenching rains.

Added to this the people became bewildered for at this time Irish was spoken in the rural districts of Ireland and barely understood. No attempt was made to explain anything to them and the destitute were treated with contempt. This seemed to heighten the traditional English distrust and dislike for the native Irish.

The first to succumb were the poorest of all who had put up a hut of soils in a bog. With their potatoes lost they abandoned their huts of sod and descended on the towns in droves, half starving, sleeping in ditches or doorways. Those in Cork alone died at one hundred a week.

Tara sat with a blanket around her, near the turf that glowed and gave heat to the fireplace. Patrick, taller now, and lanky, ran through the door.

"Father Boyle wants to see you right away."

She had no idea why and was not too happy to trudge through the snow with the thick blanket around her, but it was warmer than her threadbare coat. She donned her scarf around her head and put on her boots.

She heard the neighing of a few horses in Father Boyle's barn. He must have bought a second one, though she could not imagine why or how he could afford one.

He greeted her at the door and hugged her hard.

"I have a surprise for you. You have a visitor in the bedroom down the hall."

"A visitor? Me?"

"I'll take your scarf, your coat and your boots."

She walked slowly down the hall. What if it was someone she didn't care to see?

She looked into the room. John McGuire stood before her.

"John!"

She placed her hand on her chest, half in shock.

He ran across the room and kissed her passionately, as she did him. She had never known such feelings surging through her body before and felt certain she would fall if he let her go.

"I love you so much," he whispered. "More than I've ever loved any woman."

"I love you too," she said, as they kissed passionately again.

Finally, they broke away.

"But surely you know you're in such danger. There's a large reward out for you. And I just found out a few days ago that from now on British ships will have two armed guard on them."

"How did you find this out?"

"I—I overheard it in the tea room. It was two British officers."

"You've given me some important information."

He kissed her again. Finally, she slumped into the nearest chair.

"I've come to ask you something. Will you marry me? Let's face it, I'm facing a dangerous life; and if, God forbid, I do wind up dying, I want it to be as your husband."

She frowned.

"I'm so afraid for you. Every day. But yes, yes, of course I'll marry you."

"I've already spoken to Father Boyle about it. He said he would marry us tomorrow, at eight o'clock in the morning. I'll have to leave in the morning before anyone awakens and may recognize me, especially the British, of course. But, unfortunately, I've become a kind of Irish hero, and it will travel like wild fire that I'm here. They'll be breaking down Father Boyle's door to shake my hand. We'll have no real honey moon, of course, except that one night together." He smiled. "And I know no self-respecting Irish Catholic girl would sleep with a man unless she was married."

She blushed.

A knock at the door sounded.

"I've made a meager dinner for you," Father Boyle said.

They devoured it; some bread, some soup made from nettles he had gathered and he surprised them with a small piece of meat he had been saving and cut it in thirds.

The rest of the evening was spent talking mostly about the famine. Tara had to leave before complete darkness set in for she knew her father and brother would wonder about her if she was very late.

McGuire took her in his arms.

"I'll see you tomorrow at eight, my darling."

"Yes, yes. I can't wait." She donned her scarf, boots, coat, and left.

She did not feel the cold as she walked the ten minute pathway home, only the memory of the warmth of John McGuire's body holding her in his arms.

John Maguire lay on the cot Father Boyle had provided for him and could not sleep. Was he doing the right thing marrying Tara when he could be killed any day now? Was that fair to her? He wished so hard he had a close brother to council him, but his dearest friend had said he definitely should marry her. And he supposed he was right. How could this have happened to him? He thought of himself as rather strong, mature, and level-headed. Yet, from the moment he had seen Tara he was in love and knew it. He had been with so many women during the times they traveled the country, not to mention his youth, but when he looked at her it was as though he felt completely defenseless. And it wasn't just her great beauty. It was when she volunteered for the dangerous task of distracting the captain of the ship they were raiding that night. She seemed so utterly fearless in her love of Ireland. As fearless as he was in defending his country. Most women he had known knew so little of the political situation at the heart of the conflict, but he was willing to bet she had been following it day to day in the newspapers. He felt somehow bonded to a woman like this. He had known so many beautiful but frivolous types. He had dreams of Tara, of their future together; perhaps when it was all over (and it must be!) they might get a small farm, raise some animals, grow a potato crop, have beautiful children, which was his greatest dream. He wondered how she would feel about that. Why, of course she would want children. If only things worked out as planned, they would have a wonderful life together. No more negative and depressing thoughts, he vowed. He could not wait until he could make her completely his.

Tara thought the next day was the longest of her life. Every minute seemed an eternity as she dressed and waited for the time to approach nine.

She put on her best dress, the one with the roses embroidered around its neckline and her mother's dress shoes. Then she placed a dab of berry blush on her cheeks. She had snipped the ends of the large pine tree adjacent to their house the night before and wired them together to form a crown for her hair. Patrick and her father would not attend. It would be too dangerous if anyone saw them entering Father Boyle's home with

Tara in what looked like a wedding garment. McGuire must be protected at all costs.

She heard a joyous sigh from McGuire as he stood in the room where they were to be married, looked at her, then took her hand.

Father Boyle appeared in a long white and gold garment covering his cassock.

He smiled at them.

"Shall we begin? Since we are unable to have a complete Mass with the offering of Communion and responses from the laity, I have omitted them." He smiled again. "But I assure you that you will be husband and wife when the ceremony is completed. John, will you please step forward and stand to the right side of the bride?"

He did as Father Boyle asked. A plump-faced woman with rosy cheeks, Father Boyle's housekeeper, entered.

"Mrs. Hatch will act as the bride's matron of honor. He motioned to Sean McCullough, John's best friend and bodyguard, his hair combed back and straight as wire, with a quivering lip, to step forward. "And Sean will act as best man."

She now understood why she heard more than one horse neighing in Father Boyle's barn. McCullough must have slept in there all night.

Father Boyle began reading from the prayer book he held:

"John McGuire, will you take Tara O'Brien, here present, for your lawful wife, according to the rite of our holy Mother, the Church?

He responded, "I will."

Tara O'Brien, will you take John McGuire, here present, for your lawful husband, according to the rite of our holy Mother, the Church?"

She responded, "I will."

John then took Tara's left hand, and, prompted by Father Boyle, promised her his troth.

"I, John Mc Guire, take you, Tara O'Brien, for my lawful wife, to have and to hold, from this day forward, for better, for worse, for richer, for poorer, in sickness and in health until death do us part."

Tara responded, "I, Tara O'Brien, take you, John McGuire, for my lawful husband, to have and to hold, from this day forward, for better, for worse, for richer, for poorer, in sickness and in health, until death do us part."

Father Boyle made the sign of the cross.

I join you together in marriage in the name of the Father, the Son, and the Holy Spirit. Amen."

Sean removed a gold wedding ring from his pocket and handed it to Father Boyle.

Father Boyle began:

"Bless, O Lord, this ring, which we bless in Your name that she who is to wear it, keeping true faith to her husband, may abide in Your peace and obedience to Your will, and ever live in mutual love, Through Christ our Lord. Amen."

He then sprinkled the ring with holy water in the form of a Cross; and John, having received the ring from the hand of Father Boyle, placed it on Tara's ring finger of her left hand and she said:

"With this ring I wed you and I pledge you my fidelity."

At that time Father Boyle then spoke:

"In the name of the Father, the Son, and the Holy Spirit.

The Gospel According to Matthew 19, 3-6 "At that time there came to Jesus some Pharisees, testing Him, and saying, "Is it lawful for a man to put away his wife for any cause?" But he answered and said to them, "Have you not read the Creator, from the beginning, made them male and female, "For this cause a man shall leave his father and mother and cleave to his wife, and the two shall become one flesh"? What, therefore, God has joined together let no man put asunder."

He then closed the holy book, and said "Congratulations" to both of them.

They kissed rather demurely.

Sean smiled at John and said, "Well, now you are an old married man."

"And I couldn't be happier."

John and Tara were beaming.

A few minutes later Father Boyle appeared with a small traveling case as did Sean McCullough.

"We thought we'd leave the two of you alone for the rest of the time you have together. As you know Maureen O'Flanagan's house is now vacant so we'll stay there tonight and into morning to give you and Tara some time for yourselves."

"That's good of you both," John said.

They had another light dinner and then Sean and Father Boyle left for the evening.

John McGuire had never truly been afraid in his life, as far as he could remember. But now he was terrified. He had been with many women in his life but this was a different situation. First of all, he loved Tara more than he ever thought he could love a woman and secondly, he knew she was a virgin. How would she react to the sex act? Perhaps she would be submissive for his sake, not enjoying it at all. He would have to control himself completely and he worried about that because he loved her so much. He wondered how much she really knew about the sex act. Obviously, her father or Patrick had never mentioned it. And what he knew of her mother she was a demure, rather shy person.

Perhaps they shouldn't have sex at all; after all, it was their first night together and it might be better to eventually lean into it. It might be better for her that way. But, then again, they were married now and she knew there was nothing 'wrong' with it. He supposed he would just have to take the lead from her, in a sense, and see how she seemed to be feeling about it.

Tara and John, Father Boyle and Sean McCullough stayed a time after the ceremony. Father Boyle tried to serve some food and drink from what he had on hand, which wasn't very much. They kept insisting it was quite all right. John did most of the talking, hoping to prolong the time he and Tara would finally be alone. But soon enough the time came for Father Boyle and Sean to depart.

After they left, Tara said, "I want to make love to you. I—don't know much about it—but I know how much I want you."

"That you want to make love to me— Those are the most beautiful words I've ever heard."

"I'm sure you've been with so many other women," she frowned, "and I'm afraid I'll be such a disappointment to you."

"But you're forgetting a big difference here. I didn't love any of them. Not one bit. Not the way I love you."

"And you could never disappoint me. Just to hold you in my arms will mean more to me than the sex I've had with other women, believe me."

They undressed slowly and lay beneath the sheet. John took her in his arms; and, though he was already ready to enter her, he held back and kissed her passionately. His hand explored her wetness. He was grateful for that. She was obviously more than ready to make love to him. When he did enter her after a few minutes, she began to moan and her whole body quivered. He knew it was most likely the first time she'd had an orgasm. His sexual desire culminated soon after.

Moments later they lay, holding each other tightly, feeling in a state of euphoria.

"That was the most wonderful feeling my body ever knew," she sighed. "No wonder so many people make such a fuss about sex. Can we do it again?"

He laughed, "Well, we have to wait a while. But I'm so glad I satisfied you."

"That you did," she smiled. "That you did."

Eventually they fell asleep in each other's arms.

In the early morning they had sex again in the semi-darkness, both realizing they had no idea when they would see each other again. The morning had come too soon and she could see Sean McCullough in front of the church, waiting for John. He slept so peacefully she hated to wake him but she knew the danger he could face if he were recognized in daylight. Her heart felt like shattered glass at the thought of his leaving and that he could be injured or even killed. When would this damned famine end?

She woke him and he quickly got dressed. "I don't know when we'll see each other again. There's a ship in the bay we plan to attack tonight, loaded with food the British are sending to England for profit."

She grasped his arm hard.

"Please, be careful. The British will be on that ship, at least a few of them. And armed."

"I promise I'll be careful. I'll send a message through Father Boyle when we can meet again."

He kissed her hard and held her tightly.

"Now don't go worrying about me. I've been through worse than this. I'll see you again. Sooner than you think."

He left her, mounted his horse, waved goodbye and rode off into the distance with Sean, her beating as though it would break against her ribs.

She put her coat on, donned her shoes and walked home, bereft in one way but yet a part of her filled with such joy and happiness.

When she arrived home, Tara quietly lay in her cot until Patrick shook her.

"Where in God's name were you? We were worried sick about you."

She smiled at him.

"I'm so happy. I got married."

"What? Got married? Who in the world to?"

"John McGuire."

"You mean the leader of the Irish rebellion?"

"Yes. But you mustn't tell a soul."

He hugged her and kissed her cheek.

"I won't. I swear. I don't even know if da realized you were gone. He's in his own world you know."

"We can never send him to the filthy asylum but just make do."

"Of course not. But I think we'd better keep more of an eye on him."

"I think so too. I'm hoping when the famine is over he'll come back to himself."

"How I pray that will happen."

They gathered themselves together and readied themselves to face another day of challenges of the famine.

That winter the first to succumb were the poorest of all, the 'squatters' who had no means of existence but their small crop of potatoes, and when the potatoes rotted they abandoned the small huts they lived in and entered the towns in large groups. Five thousand beggars roamed the streets of Cork; Galway had hundreds of them wandering aimlessly through the town as well as Tipperary and other towns, sleeping in ditches and doorways, begging, and were driven away. Those in Cork alone died a hundred a week.

Far more serious was a change in the type of labor employed. The original plan was to employ able-bodied men and to give them a fair day's work for that day's wages. But since destitution was the criteria for employment it proved impossible to refuse destitute women, especially widows with families they had to feed. Women were the ones employed in the works, mostly shattering stones and also, old, feeble and very young people were allowed employment. Hordes of suffering, half starved women, the old and feeble, and children, completely unfit for manual labor ended any hope of discipline between men and women.

In desperation seed oats as well as the seed for corn were being eaten and the farmers asked what was the sense of preparing the ground for the spring and summer crops when there is going to be no seed? Urgent petitions were sent to the British government for seed of any kind. All were refused. Shortage of seed, of course, was not the only reason why the land was not cultivated. The Irish farmer knew the landlord would have no guilt in taking ownership of his harvest if he owned rent.

Wages on the works were only a few shillings a week, which would only give one meal a day to a family of six. In the bitter weather crowds of half starving men, women and children huddled at the works. For some months, if a day's work was impossible, a day's pay was lost. Finally, in December, a circular was issued saying half a day's wages be paid when weather stopped work; but even so early morning roll call, which frequently required a walk in snow and sleet for several miles, must be met.

Snow continued to fall; reports from inspectors for December recorded snow and gales throughout Ireland from Donegal to Wicklow, to Dublin where roads were blocked and work everywhere stopped. In Mayo the snow was so deep that the works could not even be seen.

Finally, humanitarians and philanthropists, after seeing the horror of Irish men, women, and children beginning to lie dead in the streets, formed committees and raised subscriptions for Irish relief.

They first focused on the remote districts and then later extended all over Ireland.

The Central Committee had decided to finance the establishment of food kitchens—the Quakers had experience in managing soup kitchens for the English poor. Only those who received no relief or inadequate relief from the British were to be helped.

They were shocked when they found out what was happening. The destitution and suffering was so much greater than they thought. The public works were in no way saving the people from starvation because of the enormous rise in food prices. Some were eating a turnip a day. Many of the Irish were hardly able to crawl, existing on Indian meal some days or a little cabbage and at other times nothing at all. Tara lived in a state of fear much of the time worrying about McGuire but did her best to carry on.

Miss Rouche sat quietly in her empty shop. She began to reminisce about her childhood in Marseilles. She dreamed of the French summers and the wonderful sunflowers blooming everywhere, golden in the sun, and the olive trees with their distinctive scent, the apricot trees as well. And the porches of all of the houses filled with buckets of tomatoes along with those growing in their gardens, soon to be ripe and ready for the people to can delicious tomato sauces to last through the winter, and, of course, the lavenders bushes soon ready to be picked to make lavender ice cream.

Her father was a jacquard weaver and would often bring home samples of fabric that were flawed with what the trade called "floats." Her mother always made good use of them, creating pillows or curtains, depending on the size of the fabric. And so she was always around these beautiful pieces of the weaver's craft. She dreamed of the day she would have her own shop, but there were so many in Marseilles, and in France in general. She decided to take the gigantic and for her at the time somewhat terrifying job of going to England where French fashion was all the rage with the very wealthy. The shop became an amazing success from its very beginning. Until now. And how had she become so fortunate to find a seamstress like Tara O'Brien? She could easily have opened her own shop if circumstances were different.

And now she felt utterly depressed at the news she had to bring. She called her from the back room of her shop where she was doing some sewing on a dress for one of their customers. She looked so sad when she saw Tara.

"I have to tell you something which I hate doing. I'm afraid I'm going to have to lower your salary three shillings."

Tara's eyes widened. Didn't Miss Rouche realize the implication of that.? Her salary was all they had to live on, and they barely had enough to live on with that.

"I've lost so many customers with the famine. I'm sure you noticed. I deal mostly with middle and upper class women who need a special dress for a special occasion. All that has stopped now. They are saving every shilling for bare necessities. It would be lovely if all my customers were as well to do as Mrs. Litchfield but, alas, that's not the case. Plus fabric has doubled in price since the famine. If the situation doesn't change with the potato crop come spring, I'm afraid I'm going to have to let you go altogether, much to my regret, believe me."

She had grown so fond of her. Not only was she a beautiful girl but also she was so kind and good. And who knows? Perhaps she and Captain Litchfield would marry, which would be wonderful. She was beginning to think of Tara as the daughter she never had and had plans to leave the shop to her when she died. But that wasn't of much help now that they were in the midst of a famine.

Tara slumped down in the nearest chair.

"A dress shop like this is the last place I would have thought I would ever be in danger of losing my job because of the famine. So many wealthy people buy here."

How would they ever get along? They lived on the barest essentials now.

"Well, we have to hope for the best next year. The famine can't last forever."

"Let me get back to work, Miss Rouche. I appreciate you keeping me on."

Now Tara lived in a worse state of turmoil between worrying about McGuire and now this drastic decrease in her salary. She prayed every night God would also put an end to the terrible suffering she saw around her every day. If it hadn't been for Patrick, who had discovered a spot the limpets were drawn to, and some mussels and nettles he was able to retrieve, still growing miraculously beneath the snow, or once in a while some birds' nest eggs they would surely have starved, along with the loaf of bread she was still able to purchase each week. Then she discovered her rent, plus some money for extra food, was being paid by an anonymous donor. She knew, of course, it was Captain Litchfield and wrote him a letter thanking him for his charity, which she knew they needed desperately. But her guilt at accepting it never left her.

One evening when, as usual, she lay awake thinking of John and praying to God to keep him safe, she smelled something burning. She quickly ran to her father's cot which was partially aflame and noticed his pipe on the floor. She grabbed a blanket and ran to his cot, smothering the flame. But it was too late and the fire was out of control as her father stood there, immobile, watching the flames.

She ran to Patrick's cot, woke him up.

"The house is on fire! Ride to the fire brigade down the way as fast as you can. "He dressed in seconds, took a moment to see the blazing cot, and was gone.

It took quite a few minutes for the men on the brigade to dress and check that the water pumps were filled to capacity and harness the horses. When they arrived and used the giant fire pumps filled with water, the fire finally got under control.

After they left, Tara and Patrick stood there in disbelief, their father standing and staring, in his other world.

She began to cry.

With so much else on her mind, she had to cope with this fear as well, that he would inadvertently set another fire. She finally gained control.

"At least we have a roof over our heads and the damage isn't that bad. But we were lucky this time. I think eventuaally we'll have to build a shale like so many others and have to live in it. "It would have to be dug in the earth about ten feet and covered with woven branches to keep out the rain and cold."

"I don't think we're at that point yet."

"You're right. I'm not thinking straight, Patrick." She squeezed her forehead with her fingers. She thought of Captain Litchfield who was still paying their rent.

The neighbors who had gathered around at hearing the bell began to disperse to their cottages or shales.

She must think.

"Father Boyle! We know he has extra cots. He would surely take us in for the night."

A sleepy-eyed Father Boyle answered his door.

"Oh, father, the worst thing has happened and my da's cot got burned to a crisp. And his arms are all burned too."

"Blessed Jesus! You are all to stay here tonight. I have some bread. Don' t ask me how I got it but I'm sure the Lord will forgive me."

He went to the back area of his cottage where he had a smalll kitchen and gave the three of them a good sized piece of bread, which they devoured.

Tara's was to sleep in Father Boyle's bed while Patrick and Liam could sleep on cots on the floor.

"Now all of you try to get some sleep. We'll talk about this in the morning"

Later, Tara could hear her father snoring and see Patrick fast asleep, while she lay most of the night wondering what ever would become of them.

And then she made her decision.

At breakfast she told Sean of her fears of their father doing worse damage. And so, with much sadness in their hearts, they decided they must bring him to the lunatic asylum.

The lunatic asylum was in Armagh, not that far from where Tara lived and so they decided to walk. She packed her father's bag with a few shirts, an extra pair of pants, and other basic necessities.

When they arrived at St. Theresa's Lunatic Asylum, they were very impressed by its cleanliness. The gray stones it was comprised of were very clean as well as the windows.

They rang the bell and a nun answered.

"I'm Sister Bernadette. May I help you." She had a lovely face, which looked like it had a permanent smile on it, and her wimple and other garments were spotless.

"We'd like to inquire if we can let our da stay here."

"Won't you come in?"

She led them to her office which was immaculately clean but possessed worn furniture.

"Would you mind waiting for us outside, Mr. O'Brien?"

Tara and Patrick's father left the room, closed the door.

"Can you tell me what the problem seems to be?"

"Well," Tara began. "I think it all started when our mother died, not too long ago. But da was able to go on because he had the potato crop to cope with. But then with the coming of the famine he seemed to go into a daze. He just sat on our tiny porch or the fence and stared into space. He also stopped talking, but we put up with it thinking once the famine was over he would come back to his senses. We were very lucky we had—a—friend who paid our rent and gave us money for food."

"You certainly were," she smiled.

"But then one night when I was in bed and couldn't sleep, I smelled smoke. I ran to da's bed and saw him sitting up watching the flames as the fire was burning his bed and bedclothes. We went to report the fire and while we waited filled buckets of water to try to douse the flames, But we couldn't. Finally, thank the Lord, the fire truck arrived and put it out. It was then we knew we had to do something about da. The cottage could of burned down and we could of been burned to death. That's when we decided with us not being home all the time, he had to go to the asylum. And he understood that."

"I think you made a very wise choice."

She stood up.

"Let me show you his room."

She led them down the hall toward his room.

"I couldn't help notice your beautiful daffodils," Tara commented. "And I see you have eight rose bushes scattered here and there. They're my favorite. They should start to bloom before you know it."

"Yes, we're very lucky Sister Clementine seems to have a green thumb and really enjoys tending the garden area."

They reached his room. She opened the door and they were very disappointed. The walls were a pea soup green and had many chips, the coverlet was faded from so many washings as was the pillow on the rocking chair. A plain lamp, which once looked as though it once had a flower design on it, sat on the worn dresser. Tara noticed there were a few holes in the now-faded flowered rug. There was a vase of daffodils on top of the dresser.

"I know you must be disappointed in the room. Everything is so worn. But you see we get so few donations to update things. Once people see the word "lunatic" they think of completely hopeless cases and I think they get a sense of fright as well. Of course we do have some seriously ill people in the south side of the building, but I can assure you we have had many cases of people who are able, after a time of good care, to come home again. It's sad that people don't think of mental illness as seriously as they do heart disease or gout, or the more common illnesses. If they could only know the suffering these poor souls go through."

"I can tell you're a very kind person, Sister. And I am very glad we spoke with you. I think my da will be treated very well here."

"I thank you," she smiled.

After they hugged, her father entered, and Sister Bernadette spoke with him a time,

"You can be sure we'll visit him as much as we can to see how he progresses," Patrick offered.

"That would be wonderful. So many of our patients never receive a visitor at all."

Tara and Patrick left in a sad state, but they also knew they had done the right thing.

The morning began and they awoke to a glorious, atypical day. Cardinals and sparrows were chirping in the trees. The sun was beating down upon the emerald grass as well at Father's Boyle's cottage and Tara and Patrick paid him a visit. They even had a breakfast of a piece of bread, Tara feeling especially guilty because it would be one less piece for Father Boyle.

"I've been thinking," he began, "Why don't you take a cot from Maureen O'Flanagan's cottage? It's a wonder no one's taken it over but I suppose she'll eventually be back here again. And I know she wouldn't mind. I keep hoping she'll write to you, Tara, and you can tell us all the news of America. I hear America's a wonderful place. And I know, with you being her best friend and the circumstances you're in now, she'd be glad of it."

"Father Boyle, you surely are a lifesaver. I can get Patrick and a few of his friends to carry it over to our cottage today."

John McGuire was readying himself for another attack on a British ship. So far they had been unbelievably successful. Whoever would have thought as a little boy this would be his lot it life? His mother had been sweet and loving and when she died he missed her dearly. He thought about her almost every day and the abuse his drunken father put the four boys through after a night of drinking. Yet, they bore up to it. They had no choice. Their father had always thought they would all follow in his footsteps and become farmers as he had. That is exactly what happened, except for John. He wanted to travel and see the world. And so he had a variety of jobs for six years until he had enough saved to fulfill his dream., He had seen China, Japan, France, Germany, Switzerland and finally came to the conclusion there was not one place as appealing as the one he loved most, Ireland.

When he returned, he worked for a few years as an apprentice in a blacksmith shop and enjoyed the work; but he felt more and more drawn to an occupation where he could help people. Teaching was his first choice, but all those years of having to work to be certified did not appeal to him. When the famine struck, he had no thought of being actively involved with it; but as it became worse and worse, he finally realized what his calling was, though he had to idea how he would carry it out. One day he heard the man who was to become his best friend, Sean McConnell, making a speech about the British and their role in the famine. He knew from that moment on what his role should be. He introduced himself to McConnell and from then on they became the best of friends. He also found he had a gift of oratory, so strong he was able to move people to action by his words. And from those few speeches he arose to become the leader of the Irish rebellion against the British, finally to such a point he had to obtain three other men to be his bodyguards wherever he went. The work was extremely dangerous but he thrived on it, knowing he was helping the suffering and starving. So far he and his friends were very successful. His father had disowned him when he told him he had no interest in farming and was going to travel until he could finally get grounded in what he wanted to do with his life. When he met Tara, his thoughts of a single loner's life were shattered. He would eventually, he hoped ironically, go back to the land—and with her.

McGuire and his bodyguards plus twenty other men who had joined their group had made an unbelievably successful raid on the "Queen Victoria" the week before and were now riding to Skibbereen. He had heard the very worst hardships were there so that was their target, to bring the pillow cases filled almost to the brim with meal to them, and most astoundingly, some had meat. They arrived in darkness.

"Remember," McGuire said, "make the twenty families you distribute to take the oath that, in the name of Jesus Christ, they share it with as many families as possible." And off they went. John usually hid in one of the cottages in Skibbereen, so that he did not draw attention for wherever he was seen crowds would surround him and want to shake his hand and thank him.

However, this time, he, along with Sean said, "I want to see for myself what's happening here. I've heard so many stories of the conditions here and I want to

see if they are true. I want to see with my own eyes
the accounts that the starvation in the western part of
the country are worse than the east. If so, we have to
concentrate on there when we raid the British ships."

They entered some of the hovels, or shales, and the
scenes he and Sean saw were so horrible a tongue or
pen could scarcely describe them. In the first shale he
saw starving and horrifying skeletons, dead, huddled
in a corner on dirty straw, their sole blanket ragged
horsecloth, their thin legs laying naked above their
knees. He then realized they were not quite dead, and
as he approached with shock, found by the low moaning
heard they were alive—four children, a woman and
what had once been a man. He left the shale going to
the others and saw at least two hundred men, children,
and women, who looked like ghosts caused by famine
or fever. Their calls for help echoed in his ears and
he knew their ghastly images would be fixed in his
brain always. Their clothes were mainly torn off as
they tried to escape the pestilence around. They seized
his neckcloth and he turned to face a woman with an
infant just born. They opened a house, locked for many
days and found two frozen corpses of her child, a girl

about five, perfectly naked, leaving it on the ground, half covered with stones.

Deaths were occurring daily; almost two hundred Irish had died in the workhouse, and one hundred bodies had been eaten by rats.

Suddenly, John McGuire felt dizzy.

"Take me cross country to the safety of Father Boyle," he said, "This is too much for me."

Though Sean was just as depressed, he managed to go to the cottage where he distributed the food and told them they would be in touch. They must never see a weakness in their leader.

McGuire and McCullough rode slowly. John was breathing heavily when they arrived at Father Boyle's. He let them in quickly, sensing the state McGuire was in.

"Father, John's not doing his best," Sean offered. "We've just come from Skibbereen."

Father Boyle led him to the back room, laid him on a cot.

John's eyes appeared glazed. He ran his fingers through his hair. "The things I saw in Skibbereen."

Father Boyle placed a light blanket over him. "They say that's the most hit."

"We brought them twenty bags of food."

"I'm sure they'll thank you forever for that."

"But it's hardly enough. Dear God, the things I saw. The things I saw."

He sat up on the cot.

Father Boyle called Sean to the side.

"Try to explain the situation to Tara when she arrives. He needs to rest."

Father Boyle and Sean came back into the room.

"Lie back down, John. Try to get some rest. You've completely overdone yourself."

"The things I saw," he moaned. "The things I saw."

After a few minutes he closed his eyes and fell into a deep sleep.

Dr. Beel, a craggy faced, thin man with kind brown eyes and hanging jowls," had been the family doctor in Monaghan for over thirty years now.

When it was Tara's turn, which took over an hour since the office was always filled with patients, he took one look at her and asked her to remove her blouse and skirt. This surprised her because she had been feeling sick every morning and weak. She thought perhaps she was catching the flu, or a fever.

He examined her thoroughly.

"It's not the famine fever, is it, doctor?"

"No, it isn't."

"Tara, when did you have your last period?"

She blushed.

"I wondered about that. It's been about three months, closer to four."

"Yes, that makes sense. These times are so hard, I know. Nevertheless, I'm happy to tell you you're going to have a baby."

She felt she would fall off the cot she was lying on.

"Have you been feeling sick in the morning, not like yourself, with throwing up at times?"

"Yes, I have. But I thought it might be the beginning of the famine fever or a cold."

"Well, thank heaven it isn't." He smiled. "And I'm sure a beautiful woman like you will have a beautiful child. You're married to John McGuire, aren't you? He's a great man, has done so much for the Irish people. He'll be thrilled knowing he'll have a son or daughter. That is, if you catch up with him."

"I never thought I could love anybody as much as I love him. I don't see him as much as I'd like, but I know he's busy helping the people of Ireland in their great need. I'm so proud of him."

She opened her change purse.

"How much do I owe you, doctor."

"Nothing. Your husband has more than repaid me with his good works."

"Bless you doctor," she said as she was leaving.

When Tara walked home, she was in a frightened state. A baby. She felt her heart had been cut by a sliver of glass. She didn't know a thing about babies being born. Her mother, Kathleen, was so shy she had to read about the sex act in the library. And now she was having a baby! How in the world could a baby's head and body emerge from that small opening in her vagina? And she had no one to ask. Certainly not Patrick. Oh, why had Maureen moved to America? She probably knew about such things. And then she thought of the one person she could always talk to, Father Boyle.

She knocked on his door, he opened it, and she burst out crying.

"Come in! Come in!" he said, seeing her despair.

"What is it, my dear?"

"I just came from the doctor. I'm going to have a baby. I'm over three months pregnant."

"That's wonderful! Wonderful!"

"But I'm so frightened. How is a big baby going to come through—that opening?" She blushed as she pointed to her vaginal area.

"Didn't Kathleen, I mean, your mother explain to you about these things?"

"She was too shy to talk about them, I think."

"Well, then I'll tell you about the basics of them. That opening—it gets very, wide, much wider than the size of the baby," he lied. And it just slips out."

He hadn't the heart to tell her of the pain she would most likely endure. "It has what they call an imbilical cord, the doctor snips it, and it gets tied. And very basically, that's it. Now that doesn't sound so bad, does it?"

"But what about the pain and agony some women have told me about when I've heard them talking about it?"

"That?" Oh, that's if the baby weighs over fifteen pounds and rarely happens, or if it comes out feet first, which happens in one in a million births."

In his heart he prayed to the Lord to forgive his lies.

Tara sighed. "I feel much better now."

She left him in a much calmer state than when she had arrived.

When Tara arrived home, Patrick told her he had seen John's and Sean's horse in Father Boyle's barn. When she arrived at Father Boyle's again he made a sign with his index finger to her to remain as quiet as possible. He filled her in on what had happened. When they arrived, Sean said John was not well and he immediately put him to bed. They had just come from Skibereen, had brought the people there twenty bags of food, but that area of Ireland seemed to be the hardest hit. He kept saying, "The things I saw," "the things I saw." He was totally depleted so Father Boyle had put him to bed and he was now fast asleep.

Tara peeked into the room where John lay. She saw his face was white and his eye lids looked black and blue. She quietly left, giving him time to sleep.

A few hours passed and she checked on him again. He was awake, and she lay down beside him.

"Tara, I'm not good. The things I saw. I can't get them out of my mind."

"Think about good things. Come spring the famine will surely be over, the flowers beginning to bloom. And all this horror will be over for you. We can begin to plan our lives together." She smiled at him. "Perhaps we could start out by renting a cottage, grow a good crop of potatoes, have a few horses and pigs, chickens." She blushed. "And eventually we'll have children. These are the things you must think about."

His face brightened.

"Do you really think so? Really?"

"Of course I do. I never say anything I don't truly believe. Listen I have some chamomile leaves in my pocket. I'll have Sean make you some tea and lie down beside you. I want you to have a complete rest the next few days."

"But after what I saw, I have to get back. I have to get more food for the starving."

"No. I forbid it. I'm afraid you're stuck with me, Father Boyle, and Sean the next few days," she smiled.

"I had no idea things were as bad as what I saw today. I've been mostly in the eastern part of Ireland, but I know now I have to concentrate on getting food to the people in the western part, which is much worse."

She handed him the cup of chamomile tea Sean had made and sat beside him on the cot holding his hand. When she was convinced he slept, she slowly got up and went to Father Boyle's largest room where the furze was burning and Sean was there.

Sean began to pace the room. "We must do more," he said. "John is right. We must!"

"He's sleeping now," Tara said when she entered the room. We have to keep him here for a few days, if it's all right with you, Father. No one will suspect he's here."

"Of course."

For a few days Tara tried to nurse him as best she could with the little food Father Boyle could spare. Then Sean, who was so unhinged by John's demeanor, suddenly remembered they had a pillow case filled with food tied to his horse's saddle and went to retrieve it and give it to Father Boyle.

"The Lord is so good," he said, accepting it with thanks.

At least, while he was there they would be eating hearty food they had taken from the ship they had attacked.

The evening of the fourth day, John appeared much better. She undressed, as did he, and they made love. She felt that she had touched heaven and knew he felt the same way.

Later he said, "I'm leaving tonight. I've lost too much time already."

"John, please," she begged. "Can't you wait a few more days until you are truly better?"

"I'm fine. On the contrary, I realize now I have to do more. You didn't see what I did a few days ago, thank the Lord."

"I've seen plenty. Just in this town."

"Well, then, you must understand."

"It's not as important to me as your life, God forgive me. What I said before, about the famine being over next year and us, rebuilding our lives. That's what's important too."

"I will try to think of that," he promised.

That night he and Sean left in the darkness, Tara's heart slashed to pieces. They met up with the twenty Irish peasants who were accompanying them on the raids, plus his other three Irish guards, and they planned for the next raid.

John did not know that the reason why the British government did not feel bound to send food to Skibbereen was that ample food was to be found there already. There was a market filled with meat, bread, fish, and much else. This strange contradiction occurred all over Ireland during the famine years, but the British government failed to realize the Irish no longer had any money and, therefore, it was inaccessible to the Irish wretches, many of whom now lived by the side of the road. And so the food might just as well have not existed. Those who starved in places like Skibbereen died not because there was no food but because they were jobless and had no money to buy it. Money to pay wages had quickly run out because the numbers unemployed were so unbelievably higher than expected and laborers were also left with no work. Also, prices rocketed, and the speculators made fortunes, especially out of Indian corn.

Finally there was a new and powerful organization which was beginning to help Ireland, The British Association, and their goal was to relieve the sufferers who were beyond the reach of the British government and distribute food, clothing and fuel to them, but in no case were they to obtain money. The Queen gave five thousand pounds and the group was able to give minimal relief.

Soup kitchens were also established via The Soup Kitchen Act, its object being the free distribution of soup so that the farmers could work on their own plots of ground and thus tend to produce food for the next harvest and perhaps earn small wages to help support their families. But a far more drastic bill accompanied it, a Relief Bill which followed and depended on the collection of rates to be collected which was practically impossible in a large number of districts. When the famine was raging only sixty two pounds had been collected. Six hundred destitute paupers were in the workhouse with no funds to feed them.

The introduction of soup was at first greeted with enthusiasm. There were many private persons, good-hearted souls, who kept hundreds of people alive by distributing it. But much of it turned out to be not only soup for the poor but poor soup. It was a tasteless compound and gave the peasants who drank it bowel complaints. Soup ran through them without giving any nourishment. And food was not the answer for it had risen so high in price that women and children would return home crying with grief at the lack of food they were able to receive with the wages of their husband and father.

February was the worst month of the horrible, unexpected winter. The Irish began to feel God had forgotten them. There were heavier falls of snow and fiercer gales, roads became impassable, carts could not travel, horses sank in drifts and had to be dug out. The streets and towns were filled with starving paupers. Families without food or fuel took to their beds and many perished unknown. Other horrors were reported; a woman and her two children were found dead and half eaten, a parish priest found a roomful of dead people; a man was still alive, and was lying in bed with a dead wife and two dead children, a starving cat eating another infant. When would it all end?

Tara lay on her cot, extremely cold, with one blanket around her. She felt miserable and threw up in the small back room basin that acted as their bathroom area. As usual, she was feeling guilty for Captain Litchfield was still paying their rent and leaving them just enough money for food for the month. She checked the furze in the fireplace and saw that it was very low, and she and Patrick would have to go and dig up a few feet of snow to find some furze beneath it, cut it up, and bring it home in large pails as soon as possible before the fire went out completely. She felt pangs in her stomach and weak overall but she must help. She prayed she had not contacted the "famine fever" which was now invading Ireland, along with starvation.

"Patrick! Wake up! The fire will be going out soon. We must get some furze to keep it going." He turned away from her to the other side of his cot. She shook him even harder. "Come on! Get up!"

They looked across Patrick's section of the room to the cot their father had previously sat on, dazed it seemed in the world far away he had created for himself.

They donned their clothing and tied thick bundles of newspaper around their boots, grabbed the buckets and shovels, ready to search for furze under the snow.

The wind was howling when they opened the door but they were fortunate Patrick had found an area about fifty feet away where there was furze no one had yet found beneath the snow. They trudged along until they reached it and began shoveling the snow away. And there it was! The life-saving furze they needed for warmth in their cottage. They filled their pails to the brim with it when they saw a figure bundled up and running towards them yelling, "Stop! Stop!" They did not recognize him from far away, but the closer he got, they realized it was Father Boyle.

"Tara! Don't you lift those heavy pails!"

She stood, befuddled.

"But we only have just a bit of furze left. The fire will go out!"

"I'll carry them for you."

"I'm perfectly fine."

"And I know you aren't. And don't ask me right now how I know. I want you to get to the doctor again tomorrow."

"But I can't afford it. It'll take from our food money," she said, feeling dizzy and weak but not wanting to acknowledge it.

"I'll pay for it."

"You're so kind to us, Father."

They trudged back to the cottage and threw some furze on the half-lit flames already there.

"That should do it for a few days," she said, her face pale.

"Patrick, the next time you need furze come get me with the pails and shovels."

"I will. And we thank you, Father."

In her heart Tara was grateful for Father Boyle's offer for she had not been feeling well lately but refused to acknowledge it.

Dr. Beel had been the family doctor in Monaghan for over thirty years now.

When it was her turn, which took over an hour since the office was always filled with patients, he took one look at her and asked her to remove her blouse and pants. This surprised her since she thought she was catching a cold, flu, or fever.

He examined her thoroughly.

These times are so hard, I know. Nevertheless, I'm happy to tell you you're going to have to visit me at least once a month now that you're pregnant."

She felt she would fall off the cot she lay on. Where would she get the money?

"I'm sure you've been generally feeling weaker at times, almost not like yourself, with sickness and throwing up at times in the morning?"

"Yes, I have"

"Well, thank heaven it isn't famine fever." He smiled. "And I'm sure a beautiful woman like you will have a beautiful child. You're married to John McGuire, aren't you? He's done so much for his people. And I'm sure he'll be thrilled knowing he will soon have a son or daughter. That is, if you ever catch up with him. Bless him. He's so busy helping the people of Ireland in their need."

"Yes, I know. I never thought I could love anybody as much as I love him. I don't see him as much as I'd like but I know he's so busy helping the people of Ireland in their great need. I'm so proud of him."

She opened her change purse.

"How much do I owe you, doctor?"

"Nothing. Your husband has more than repaid me with his good works."

She must remember to give Father Boyle the money back he gave her for the visit.

"Bless you, doctor" she said to him as she was leaving.

She decided to visit Father Boyle.

"I'm glad you came. And I'm so thrilled you and John will have a child. You're both such attractive people he or she will be a beauty."

"Do you think so?"

He dared not mention that he wanted to jump for joy at the thought of being a grandfather.

"And it's been at least three months since I've seen John. I want him to know."

"Rest assured you'll see him again and he'll be overwhelmed with joy."

"And from now on you're to share my food rations. You must give the baby as much nourishment as possible during these horrible times."

"Oh, Father, you're so good to me," she said as she left.

After she closed the door, he whispered:

"My daughter ... my grandchild ..."

The Irish people spoke of "famine fever" but, in truth, two diseases were present, typhus and relapsing fever, both caused by the common louse, already very familiar in Ireland. The excrement of a typhus-stricken louse can only deposit on the skin and allow invasion, without a bite, through any tiny abrasion, even when the excrement dries to a fine dust. Usually the person scratches at the bite of the louse and the skin is broken. Rickettsia enter and that is the beginning of the infection. And so infectious is the excrement of a typhus-stricken louse its mere deposit on the skin allows invasion, without a bite, through any minute abrasion. Even when the excrement has died to a fine dust Rickettria remain active and can enter through the eyes and even be inhaled. Kind and benevolent people who gave aid to the victims of the great Irish epidemic—clergy, nuns, doctors, contracted typhus and died, even though they may have never harbored a louse.

Tara prayed every night that she would not be struck by typhus and tried to stay away from other people as much as possible. She had read about how Rickittsia attacks the small blood vessels of the body, especially the skin and brain; the face swells and the person turns a very dark color which has given typhus its Irish name, "black fever." The limbs twitch violently, the person throws himself about in delirium, is in terrible pain, vomits, develops gangrene followed by the loss of fingers, toes, and feet. A terrible odor comes from his body. More than often the person will jump in the river and commit suicide.

The problem was that conditions were favorable to these illnesses. The Irish people were filthy. They had sold every piece of clothing that would give them a fraction of a penny, wearing the same dirty rags day in and day out. Most of their bedding had been sold, and they slept covered with rags and old coats. Groups of beggars and homeless paupers tramped the roads, drifting from place to place without a destination, filthy, starving and louse infested, often with fever actually on them and once an infection had been brought to a district, it spread like lightning. A brush in passing was enough to transfer the fever. Transmitting louse or its dustlike excrement to a new victim, and one fever-stricken person could pass an infection to a hundred others within a day.

Tara entered the confession box. The darkened door of the box opened and a light shined through. She could see the profile of Father Boyle as he readied to hear her confession.

"Bless me, Father, for I have sinned."

"How long has it been since your last confession?"

"Two weeks, Father. And since then a British soldier has been paying our rent and now he's sending money for our food. I feel so terribly guilty; but, of course I share whatever we have with Maureen O'Flanagan''s aunt and the family she's living with."

"If you are the same person I spoke to before about it being acceptable to have dinner with this British man, I certainly think it's acceptable for you to use the money for food during these terrible times. Plus—he hesitated—you must get the proper nourishment, no matter where it comes from. After all you're eating for two people now. And if he asks you to dinner again, say 'yes' for under the circumstances John O'Brien would understand, I'm sure."

She was taken aback. He knew who she was.

"Many people think men are ignorant of such things and that beautiful slight lump on your stomach shows God is giving a gift to you. And remember—all of this conversation is being spoken in the sanctity and secrecy of the confessional."

"Oh, Father, I'm so relieved I'm not in mortal sin. I always feel so much better when I talk to you, whether it's in or out of the confessional."

"For your penance, say five Hail Marys."

"Thank you so much, Father."

She left the confessional. Father Boyle sat there quite a time thinking, remembering ... if only she knew that she was his daughter.

But that could never be.

When Father Boyle was ordained years back, he was assigned to Bard Academy near Limerick. He taught English there—Keats, Shelley, Byron, Milton, Shakespeare and many others, as well as composition. The students loved him for his kind and gentle manner, his understanding of their sins when they confessed them. It was largely due to his presence there that the school enrollment blossomed, and during his fifth year, there were eighty more students enrolled than when he began. He had also started a sports program of baseball, basketball, and soccer. He refused to begin a football team because he felt it was too violent a sport. And, contrary to what he expected, the students seemed to respect him for it.

Then, suddenly, after five wonderful years, one day Monsignor Fitzpatrick, a kindly man with a face like crinkled parchment, called him to his office. He said he was needed elsewhere, in a town that was losing parishioners and needed as he put it in the letter Monsignor showed him, "a shot in the arm." Its enrollments in the Catholic school were down and so were the parishioners who attended Mass. The name of the town was Monaghan. Part of a priest's obligations as he accepted membership in the priesthood was to go wherever God and his superior sent him where he could best serve Him on earth.

Father Boyle swallowed hard.

"I never expected this change in assignment in a million years. I've been so happy here."

"And I must say you've worked wonders in the parish. But we must remember our happiness does not come first. It is what God wills for us."

"Of course."

"You will finish out the next two weeks that end the semester and leave a few days afterwards. I must say I will miss you personally. You have been a credit to Bard."

"Thank you monsignor. And I must say I feel the same way."

They shook hands and parted. Father Boyle did not sleep that night wondering what this strange place, Monaghan, must be like and the huge job ahead of him.

He did not realize that he would have an experience there that would change his life until the day he died.

As it turned out, Monaghan was a rather lovely place. It was the end of spring when he arrived and the grass was as green as emeralds, with yellow daffodils popping up here and there. He was nervous giving his first sermon and prayed to God to see him through. The congregation seemed pleased with it and he heard many congratulations after Mass when he greeted the parishioners outside, shaking hands with them. They seemed a lovely group of people and very welcoming. One woman with long, auburn hair, tied back, and a large straw hat, approached him with her son. They shook hands of greeting, but when she touched his hand a strange feeling of warmth surged through him and he sensed she felt it too.

"I'm Kathleen O'Brien and this is my son, Patrick. I must say I thought your sermon was wonderful. I liked the idea of faith, that all will work out in the end if we have faith in God. No matter what the circumstances, we have control of our world, where God lives, with his eternal reassurance giving us inner peace." She paused, then said, "I needed to hear that. and I thank you. I'm looking forward to hearing your future sermons."

Something within him said "danger" when she spoke, but it passed.

Yet, each time Sunday came he looked forward to seeing her. A few months later, she invited him for tea and cake. He saw that their cottage was very small and couldn't imagine how they could get by in such small space. It was decorated with lovely lace curtains that brightened the room a great deal and a bunch of daffodils was on the table. He noticed a cot, which must be where their son slept.

Her husband stood next to her.

"Liam, I'd like you to meet Father Boyle, the new priest in our parish."

They shook hands but he did not speak.

The conversation was basically light and airy. He talked about his last assignment and how much he had enjoyed it. He found himself staring at her more and more, her lovely auburn hair tinged with gray fell beneath her shoulders, and her green/gray eyes showed an alertness in her. She was truly listening to his every word.

"Do you think there's a chance we can start a baseball team, father?"

"Why, that's a splendid idea. We had one at Bard and I was the coach, for better or for worse."

They smiled, except for Liam who hadn't said a word the whole time but was very happy to help himself to a second piece of chocolate cake.

As the afternoon ended, he realized he had to prepare for evening Mass.

Kathleen led him to the door.

"I'm sorry about my husband, Father. He isn't a believer, you see. He rarely comes to church.""

She took his hand in hers. He felt as though a flame was permeating his body and he sensed she felt the same way.

"I must tell you something. I thought perhaps it would wear away as the months have passed, but it's become worse. It's one of the most terrible of sins because you're a priest, but I'm in love with you, she whispered. I think it was the moment I saw you. It's awful, I know."

"I—can't respond to that."

"I understand. Of course. But I had to tell you. I had to. It's been on my mind for months."

How he longed to tell her he felt the same way and thought he would die unless he could hold her in his arms, kiss her, love her.

Instead, he said, "Thank you so much for the tea and cake. And a lovely afternoon."

And then he walked through the door, and was gone.

They fought their feelings for months and after Mass she left immediately to return home without speaking to him. Yet, they both knew that, as much as they tried to ignore their feelings, they would eventually have a sexual relationship. He was excited yet terrified by the thought of it for, of course, he was a virgin and knew little to nothing about how to satisfy a woman. Why, he had never even masturbated in his life, for it was a mortal sin. And here he was—a priest—in love.

Kathleen knew it was inevitable that some day they would have a sexual relationship. One day when his housekeeper was off, she went to the rectory for she knew he desired her as much as she him.

He opened the door, let her in, closed it. He immediately took her in his arms and felt a hunger for her he had never known could exist. They undressed in his room and made love. She tried to calm down his nervousness. The moment he was inside her she knew she had succeeded and they both had a glorious orgasm. They had waited so long, fighting this inevitable moment. Father Boyle seemed somewhat dazed after the act, for he never dreamed such overwhelming pleasure could exist.

They lay on the bed, spent.

Their guilt immediately set in.

"This must never happen again," he said.

But it did for a few months.

Father Boyle went back to Bard for confession, to Monsignor Fitzpatrick. The monsignor made him vow it would never happen again, and he must never be alone with her as well. He said he would keep that promise. For his Penance, he was to say the Rosary.

Kathleen went to the priest at Mount Carmel Church, vowing to him it would not happen again. Her Penance was also to say the full Rosary. She was forgiven and was overjoyed that now she could again receive Holy Communion.

The next time they met was in the church where the nun was arranging flowers on the altar, and that was in keeping with Monsignor Fitzpatrick's saying they must never meet alone again.

"We must end this relationship," he began. "It is one of the greatest sins a priest can commit before God and I can't live with the guilt from that any longer, though, God forgive me, I'll always love you."

She stood up from the pew.

"You're right, of course. But God forgive me, I'll love you until I die."

And then she left without turning back.

A few months later, Father Boyle heard a knock at the door.

He opened it and saw Kathleen.

"A nun is arranging flowers for Mass at the church. We won't be alone. Will you meet me there in a few minutes. I would not bother you, believe me, but this is extremely important. It won't take long, five minutes."

He did as she asked.

Kathleen never tired of admiring the beauty of the church. She studied the stained glass windows of Saint Boniface, Saint Jude, Saint Theresa and the Blessed Mother, two on each side of the church. The sun was peeping through the windows and their magnificent colors seeped through the church onto them as well as some of the pews. The altar was covered with a hand-crocheted linen covering and above all was the gold sculpture of the crucified Jesus looking down on the pews. To her right were the votive candles lighted by various parishioners in memory of those who had died, who were sick, or for their own desires.

Father Thomas entered the church quickly and quietly, noticing Sister Boniface placing and arranging lilies below the statue of the Virgin Mary which stood to the front right side of the church, her vestments painted the color of the blue of the sky.

He sat down quickly as though fearful to be seen.

"Thank you for coming. I must tell you some news which I'm not sure will make you happy or sad. I'm going to have your child."

His face drained of all color.

"I'm thrilled about it. I'm three months or so along. I went to Doctor Beel yesterday. Of course, he assumes it's Liam's. But it can't be. I haven't had relations with Liam for months and months, since he went into the strange daze since the famine began. I've been wearing smocks like the one I have on now to hide any notice I might be pregnant but at three months not much shows. I am disgusted that I will have to have relations with him—and very soon—so that he and everyone else thinks the child is his. I hate the thought of it, but I must do it. After that I'll not have relationships with him again. I couldn't stand it after being with you."

"I-I don't know what to say."

"Please say you're happy about it. Please. No one will ever know except the two of us. I promise."

He stood up.

"I need time to think about this."

"Of course. I'll wait a minute or two after you leave I'll speak to Sister Boniface a few minutes."

He kneeled at the altar from his pew.

"Goodbye, Katherine. I miss you every day."

And then he left.

Katherine approached Sister Boniface.

"The arrangement of flowers looks lovely, Sister. You always do a wonderful job."

"Thank you. It's nice to know they're appreciated."

"I know they are. Well, I'd better be going. Perhaps I'll see you Sunday."

"Hopefully," she said, her face beaming with love at the task she performed.

That night, and two or three nights afterward, she had sex with Liam. He looked completely surprised when she approached him and he could tell she was in a lovemaking mood. She went through the motions, feeling nothing, but making sounds that gave him the impression she felt enjoyment. Each time it was over, she thanked God in her heart she was successful at deceiving him and hoped He knew she did it for a just cause.

Dr. Beel delivered the baby eight months later. Fortunately, she had a tuft of auburn hair and vivid green/gray eyes, features exactly like Katherine's.

Katherine named her Tara.

Father Boyle wondered why he was reminiscing about years and years ago and his conversation with Katherine in the church. So much had been happening in the present he needed the strength to endure. He had organized a group of Catholic priests and doctors whose courage during this horrible time of the famine was beyond praise. Unfortunately, deaths of the Catholic priests was common. At the coast where there was less population or chance to get food two out of three doctors who came to give aid died. Seven people died in Cavan, twelve in Connemara, four in Clifden and Galway. Forty eight died in Munster because of the fever.

The main epidemic in 1847 was typhus and relapsing fever. Dysentery was also occurring in Ireland during the famine, somewhat because the people were eating old cabbage leaves, raw turnips, and Indian meal, half cooked or raw. In Skull, dysentery was overwhelming. The people had severe abdominal pains and the food they passed was pure blood and mucus, the ground marked with clots of blood.

Scurvy was also present from lack of Vitamin C. It had been unknown in Ireland because of all the potatoes eaten, but when they rotted, it began. Gums became spongy, teeth fell out, joints became enlarged and caused tremendous suffering; legs turned black up to the middle of the thigh.

By the spring of 1847 starvation had so affected the people they became like walking skeletons. The bones of their frames were covered by something which was skin but looked more like parchment, hanging in folds. Eyes had sunk back into their head, their shoulder bones were so high that the neck seemed to have sunk into the chest, faces and neck looked like skulls. Seeing the children in these terrible conditions was worst of all. They looked like little old men and women of eighty years of age.

A curious phenomenon was the growth of hair on starving children's faces. The hair on the head fell out and grew on their faces instead. Children in County Clare had hair on their heads only in patches, but over their foreheads and temples a thick sort of downy hair grew. Sometimes the hair on their faces was as long as on their heads. No one could figure this out.

The situation was going from bad to worse. A fever epidemic hit and raged through many parts of Ireland. Alarming reports came in from all parts of Ireland. The lack of hospital accommodations for these people was disastrous. The workhouses were overcrowded and the workhouse hospitals were far too small to deal with the numbers. Almost every person was dealing with some complaint, diarrhea, extreme exhaustion, or the first stages of fever. The Central Board of Health sent doctors to inspect and report on the state of the workhouses in Cork, Bantry and Lurgan. The report was horrifying. In Cork, the state of those admitted was wretched. Many were in a dying state, and death was taking place every hour. Similar situations existed in Bantry and Lurgan.

Father Boyle received a note from John McGuire and immediately brought it to Tara. He would meet her at Father Boyle's house next Wednesday when he would be in the area. The sounds on the clock seemed eternal as she waited for the day of his arrival. Father Boyle let her in that Wednesday evening. He never ceased to look at her in amazement; she looked so much like Kathleen. When Tara saw John standing in front of her, she ran to him, clenched her arms around him, and burst into tears.

"Well, that's a hell of a greeting," he smiled.

She wiped the tears from her cheeks.

"It's just that I'm so happy to see you. It's been a while."

"We'll be attacking the "King John" in Ulster Harbor next Wednesday night and this is as close as I could get to you for now. Then we'll ride down to the Limerick area to distribute some food."

"I trust you two will have a lot of catching up to do so I'll go to my room," Father Boyle said. "Later I'll make some tea and we have those cakes you were kind enough to bring with you for me."

"I have a lot to talk to you about, Tara. I don't know if you'll like it or not."

They sat on the sofa, holding hands.

"I've made a decision. In a few months or so spring will be here, and I have a good feeling about the potato crop. A lot of the older men have told me they've lived through famines, this being the longest they can remember, and surely, come spring, the potato crop will come back,"

"Strange you should say that because da feels the same way."

"And if that happens, I won't be needed anymore." He sighed heavily. "And truth told, I'll be so glad of it not only because the potatoes will be back but because I'm exhausted, and so are my men for that matter."

Tara clapped her hands.

"That's the best news I've heard in a long time! You've saved the lives of hundreds of Irish by raiding those British ships. No one would disagree you've done more than your share.""

"I'll be thirty five next Tuesday. It's time for me to settle down, have a cottage of my own, and a plot of land to grow potatoes, vegetables, and have some animals."

'We'll have some pigs and sheep and cows. And, of course, some horses," she said, happiness gleaming in her eyes.

"You know—" he hesitated, "we never talked about it but I hope you want children."

"Of course I do."

This was her chance to tell him she was going to have a child but she felt the time was not right. All his thinking must be focused on obtaining food for the Irish and not worrying about her and the baby.

He sighed.

"Since we never talked about it before I wasn't sure you'd want them."

"I assure you I want at least ten!"

He laughed, held her closer.

"Well, maybe not ten!"

"When will your last raid on the British ships be?"

"The "King John" in Ulster harbor next Wednesday, March 17, and then our men will bring the food to

Limerick where it's needed most. That is, if all works out well."

She tightened her arms around him harder.

"Oh, John, please be careful."

"I always am."

"I heard there will be two British guards on the ships from now on."

"Where did you hear that?"

"It's from a good source. She could not tell him seen had seen Captain Litchfield and he warned her to keep away from that area. He knew her impulsive nature.

"You can't imagine the happiness I feel now, John, now that it's almost over."

"As much as I do, I'm sure."

Later, Father Boyle brought in some tea and crackers. After they finished, he left them alone.

They went to his spare room and made love so passionately both fell almost immediately asleep after the act. McGuire left early the next morning, and a sense of peace came over her knowing it would be the last time they would be separated.

The next measure they decided to try was using tents. They appeared to be satisfactory; most had boarded floors and were approved by doctors. Yet, thousands preferred to die in their own homes. Many deaths were not recorded because the Irish horror of fever even conquered the bond of family affection, which is the strongest bond in Ireland. In extreme fear parents deserted their children; neighbors who were usually kindly and generous would not cross a threshold of a cabin where fever existed; in lonely districts fever-stricken people died in their cabins, without anyone coming near them, their bodies left to rot.

The horrors taking place in Ireland were only one aspect of the fever epidemic. As the horrible months of autumn and winter passed and the failure of the potato brought starvation and pestilence, the Irish turned into a surprising direction. Before the famine, to leave Ireland had been thought to be the most terrible of fates. But now, the Irish, terrified and desperate, began to flee a country that seemed cursed. In a great mass movement they left Ireland by tens of thousands to travel the ocean to America and across the sea to Britain. But they did not leave fever behind; fever went with them; and, to their surprise the way to a new life became a path of disaster.

There was a knock on Father Boyle's door. He opened it to find Liam O'Brien standing before him. His heart pumped faster. He expected to be punched in the face any minute for Liam must have discovered somehow that Tara was not his child, but Father Boyle's.

"Might I come in Father. I won't be long. I'm home from the asylum for a week on a trial basis."

Liam surveyed the room, neat and comfortable looking. A maroon sofa sat against one wall and two moss green chairs were sitting across from it. The floor was adorned with a small, floral rug but most of it showed beautiful, polished wood. On the wall was a crucifix above the sofa and between the two chairs was a painting of the Virgin Mary. Liam could sense a feeling of guilt within him since he had never been in this room before, and certainly had been an infrequent visitor to the inside of Saint Boniface's Church.

"Would you care for a cup of tea, Liam."

"No, thank you. I'm here to ask you a favor."

"If it's something I'm capable of doing, of course."

"Yesterday I went to Dr. Beel's office. And this is strictly confidential. Right?"

"Well, it's not saying it in the confines of the confession box, but, yes, surely if you don't want anyone to know about it, you have my word."

He took a piece of paper out of his pocket.

"I knew I couldn't remember the word of what it is so he wrote it down for me."

He handed the paper to Father Boyle who read the word "dementia" on it.

"Dr. Beel explained it to me. I notice I forget most things now almost as soon as I say them, which I explained to him. I told him I wanted the full truth of it. Can I get better? Or will it get worse and worse. He told me that it most likely would get worse as time went on. It's a disease they don't know much about."

"I'm so sorry to hear this, Liam. I will pray for you."

"It's not so much prayers I wanted to ask you about. It's Tara and Patrick. If I get really bad, I would ask that you watch over them for me. For all I know I may eventually have to stay at the lunatic asylum." He frowned. "I've got to think of the facts."

"We never know what God has planned for us. But one thing I do know. I would be honored to watch over them, if it comes to the point you don't feel you can."

"In truth I haven't really watched over them for some time. At first I was forgettin' little things but now it's like I have all these tangled wires in my head and they won't get untangled."

"I understand."

"I was hopin' when the potato crop comes back, I'll be my old self again. But Dr. Beel seems to think that won't matter."

"Well, I think you should live one day at a time and do the best with what you still remember. And you have my word, if the time comes, I will watch over Tara and Patrick."

"God bless ya, Father. I feel so much better now, to know they'll have somebody there for them."

They shook hands and he left.

Father Boyle kneeled down upon the floor and folded his hands.

"Thank you, Lord. Thank you for this not being the visit I was sure it would be."

Tara sat musing about her future with John. She remembered some lovely calico in her mother's collection of all types of snippets and yardage left over from the aprons and dresses she made for her and Tara as well as some flannel for shirts for Patrick and Liam. She dug into it and found some lovely yellow calico printed with daisies which would be perfect for curtains and perhaps some seat pads for her kitchen. She could use some of the other fabric for stuffing them. She was surprised when she heard a knock on the door. It was the mailman with a letter for her. She was overjoyed to see it was from Maureen O'Flanagan, a very thick letter, so thick it had three stamps on it and was post marked Boston, Massachusetts. She was anxious to read it. From what she had heard America was a wonderful place to live, though she could never leave her beloved Ireland. She sat on the front stoop, opened it, and began to read:

Dear Tara,

I miss you so much. Coming to America was the worst thing I could have done. We don't have skills like some of the people who came over do. Because we were so poor we couldn't bring anything. Because of that with us having nothing to offer in skilled trades on the ship they put us in the lower deck which was not even fit for human beings. They call them cellar dwellings. They are dark and the floors are covered with mud. I don't see how we can ever be successful in America because we are so weak from the famine and our fate is treated with contempt and hatred. They take us because we are considered "passengers" and the British make more money based on how many are on the ship. Conveying immigrants has developed to the point where larger profits are being made by the passenger trade than by carrying timber or European goods. They are happy about that while we live in the worst conditions down below.

Once we got to America, it was hard and strange. A lot of Protestants came and anti-Catholics. They said fares have now been made higher to get to the United States. In some states passengers can't land until an official examines them, to discover if any had been paupers in another country or lunatics, idiots, maimed, aged or infirm.

All passengers had to pay two dollars 'head money' when they landed. The majority of helpless and poor people were Irish, and when we got there we landed in small coves on the coast of Massachusetts and went on by foot. Many who were said not to meet the requirements were sent back to Ireland.

Patients on the ship were often left for four or five days without any medical attention and there is only one doctor who happens to be a passenger. Nurses were not available and people were sick and suffering great torture from lack of attention. Bedding was sent down but no planks to lay it on so it became soaked with water and mud. The old passenger sheds that were relied on had never been intended for use as hospitals. They had no ventilation and the smell was awful.

The state of all the immigrants when we landed was frightening. Many got through the trip in starvation. The official weekly amount of food we get is seven pounds of food a week and it's not nearly enough. When most got here from America, they had to go to the hospital. Water also was short.

Eventually, as you can guess, ship fever broke out. The wind had dropped and the ship was only provided with enough food for that amount of time, so the captain had to hold back on our food and water.

They decided to dock at Grosse Isle but then there was a large bunch of boats, bringing the sick and dead from Grosse Isle. I saw hundreds thrown on the beach, left among the mud and stones to crawl on the dry land as best they could. Boatloads of dead were taken four times a day from a single ship. The bodies were wrapped in canvas and boxed in rough coffins made from planks and left there.

As news of the fever spread when we finally got to America, we have been dreaded by the people. They are afraid fever came with us and even if we are fit to work as I am, I couldn't find a job. Almost everyone here avoids us. Thankfully, no disaster compared to what I saw at Grosse Isle occurred in America, though there is great prejudice against us.

Because of the hatred of foreign immigration as well as anti-Catholic and anti-Irish feelings, riots have resulted in Philadelphia and Boston. I am living in New York City in an area that is all Irish, one poorer than the other. I was lucky enough to get a job as a dish washer and all my dreams of a better life in America are gone. I doubt you would ever get a job as a seamstress over here, being Irish, and you would surely never own a shop. Please write to me soon and tell me all the news of our beloved Ireland.

Love always,
Maureen

Tara folded the letter, put it in its envelope and sat stunned at what she had read. She knew she would never leave Ireland and felt certain John felt the same way. As soon as she could she would write back to Maureen.

Liam O'Brien sat on the porch of their cottage the week of his trial at home from the asylum watching the sun fall into the sky. Another day over soon. He hardly ever spoke since Kathleen died but the voices in his mind did. It seemed to him the main reason he lived was for her and now he had become a sad, lonely man, though Tara and Patrick did their best to cheer him. But soon they would marry and have their own families and he would be alone.

He began to think of the past, his favorite way to pass the days. He remembered the first time he met Kathleen when she was eighteen years old. It was at a Friday night dance in Limerick. He didn't want to go because he was a terrible dancer but his friends convinced him. His whole life might have been different if he hadn't gone for it was at that dance he met Kathleen. It was love at first sight, for him at least. He thought he had never before seen such a beautiful woman, her long, auburn hair swaying to and fro as she danced with her partner, her vivid green-gray eyes dazzling with joy. If only he had the nerve to ask her for the next dance, which was a slow one and one he thought he could manage. He finally decided he would ask her, thoroughly prepared to be rejected. But to to his shock she said yes. They made small talk as they danced. It turned out she was from Armagh, which was not very far from Monaghan, his home town. At the end of the evening after they had danced every dance together and he fell over his feet many times, he asked her if she might like to have dinner the next Saturday night. She said yes and the rest was history. He was not foolish enough to believe she was passionately in love with him. He knew his limitations ; he was a decent-looking man with good features overall, but when he told her he owned his own home and a rather large area of land she was duly impressed. What she wanted most from a man was security and knew little about love and passion because of her strict upbringing. Six months later they married and a year after that Patrick was born. She always submitted to his lovemaking, but he sensed it was out of obligation rather than a great desire for him. Yet, they were happy enough and she accepted her fate as most of her women friends did.

But she later learned there was no mistaking of desire, a desire that fell across her face when she saw Father Boyle. But they had no fear of ever having a sexual relationship not only because he was a priest but also because her religion formed the center of her life. In the beginning Liam did attend church, but when Patrick turned eight years old he felt he had given him the foundation of religious belief that was so sacred to Kathleen and he stopped attending Mass after Patrick made his Holy Communion. He was tired of putting on the act that he was a believer when he had little to no faith in the Church. Eventually Kathleen had to accept his choice though it broke her heart. The last few years had been the most difficult of his life not only because of Kathleen's death and the destruction of his dignity as the provider for his family. But also strange things were happening in his mind. He would look at his potato acreage as he did every day. The leaves were a healthy looking green as they had been in previous years. But he knew how deceiving that could be. He had been stricken with fear for the last few weeks and did not have the courage to pull out a potato from the ground for fear of the black rot again and the mush he would find rather than the beginnings of a well-formed, healthy potato. He decided today would be the day he would do it, for better or for worse. He walked over to the acreage where the potato crop grew. His hands shook as he bent down and carefully pulled a potato plant from the earth. He examined it carefully. It was strong and healthy, the size of a small plum, and showed not one sign of black rot or mushy residue that fell onto his hands.

He looked up to the heavens, then bent down on his knees.

"Thank you, Lord. Thank you!"

He ran in the house and showed Patrick, Tara and Kathleen the potato.

They jumped up and down with glee. In a month or two it would easily grow the size of a man's fist.

He and Patrick ran down to the pub to tell the men there the good news, but not before he stopped at Father Boyle's house to show it to him.

Tara had one person in mind when she saw the potato: John. It was Wednesday. the 17th day of March and that was the day John and his men were invading the "King John" merchant ship that night. She must let him know it was no longer necessary, that this would surely be the last time they would engage in raids for food with the potato crop in full, healthy growth. Plus, for days she had been thinking of the look of joy he would have on his face when she told him she was having his child.

She went to the small closet her father had built to store their clothing. She put on a pair of Patrick's pants and one of his shirts, both too big, but they would have to do. On the top of the shelf she found a woolen cap and put it on tucking her hair underneath it.

By the time she rode to the "King John" darkness had settled in. She paused for a moment to observe the ship. She knew immediately it was a merchant vessel that was rather new by the cleanliness of it. She looked at the mizzenmast which the men climbed and the ratlines reminded her of long spider webs. The length of the vessel from bowsprit to stern must have been ninety feet and the width forty feet or so. She could see the Irish men reachng the hold, filling their rowboats containing their precious supply of food and leaving. Only one was left which she was sure belonged to John. The sides of the ship were gleaming which verified her belief it had been newly painted. She observed the main mast and on top of it flew the despicable British flag, blowing in the breeze. She could see the sails were furled which meant they were likely to be in port at least a few more days.

She tied Patrick's horse to a tree. She removed her shoes and then stealthily stepped down the stairway leading to the hold where the Irish were stealing the food for her people, putting them in their rowboats and rowing away to their destination of the Irish people. The supplies the "King John" was shipping would have most likely been sold in England or some country. When she climbed to the upper deck she had seen the Irish rowboats hidden out of view near the back of the ship, most completely loaded with food and rowing away from the ship to their destination of the Irish people. One still remained. She must sneak down to the hold where John must still be for surely he would leave last.

She passed the big guns under the main deck and finally reached the hold, which was below the gun deck. She spotted John loading what looked like the last supply of food they were taking. Most of the men were gone, rowing toward shore.

"John!"

He turned as he took out his gun ready to shoot until he recognized Tara for most of her hair had fallen from her cap.

The two British officers had finally seen them and ran to the hold.

Tara hid by the side of a giant barrel and immediately recognized Thomas Litchfield as he did her. His gun was drawn and he was ready to shoot until he saw who it was. He turned away immediatley, went towards the upper deck and began trying to shoot at the Irish rowers as they fled but they were already out of range.

"You don't need to check the hold," Litchfield said. "No one's there."

"I'll just make sure." The second British soldier came down the stairs to check the hold. He could see Tara's auburn hair as he came closer for it had fallen from her cap. He shot her three times, twice in the stomach, and once in her chest near her heart. Then he was shot three times in the back by John as he ran to Tara whose body had fallen to the floor.

"Tara!"

John lifted her in his arms, tears falling upon her lovely cheeks, blood spouting from her wounds onto his shirt and pants as he held her in his arms.

Her eyes were half closed.

"Ireland," she whispered. "Ire—"

And then she died

Even to the very end she was an Irish girl.

Epilogue

The potato crop that year was wonderful. Men, women, and children held gatherings of dancing, singing, and performing the Irish jig.

There is no sorrow like the memory of love and the knowledge that it is gone forever; however, John McGuire, bereft of heart and soul, having lost weight, now thinner and haggard, after a month of inability to do anything, finally teamed up with GuyMcCullough, and became a handyman. The two of them traveled through Ireland doing odd jobs for there was much to be done due to the famine. They helped out the farmers, especially the widows who had been left behind, mending fences and barns, rebuilding stone on some of the cottages, repairing thatch roofs that leaked, birthing piglets, lambs, colts, and any other odd jobs that needed to be done. They mostly slept in the barns of the people they worked for or, if they were lucky, the extra bed in the spare room of a cottage.

Whenever they were in the area of Monagham they always stopped to see Father Boyle. He never told John that Tara was carrying his child for there is so much pain and agony a man can endure. Then they always visited Tara's grave. Each time they came, whether the budding of spring, the blossoming of flowers in summer, the myriad of colors of autumn leaves or the frost of winter, there was always a bouquet of fresh red roses upon it. They wondered who would be who placed them there so faithfully. Usually when they visited the cemetery no one else was there. Except for today. They observed a tall, handsome man walking down the path towards the exit. He wore black high boots, navy blue pants, and a red coat embellished with gold braid and an insignia that noted he was a lieutenant. His face was a mask of sorrow. But, of course, he could not be the one who placed the roses there. He was British.

They kneeled down and said their prayers for Tara at her grave and lingered a time. John kissed her gravestone. Then they both rose, crossed themselves, and moved on...

Bibliography

RENNER, MARYANN (A THESIS) 19TH CENTURY MERCHANT SHIPS, DECEMBER 1987 APPROVED BY DL HAMILTON, DAVID CARLSON, VAUGHN JUNIOR, AND CLARK E ADDAMS

SAINT JOSEPH DAILY MISSAL: THE OFFICIAL PRAYERS FOR THE CATHOLIC CHURCH FOR THE CELEBRATION OF DAILY MASS, NEW YORK 1952 CATHOLIC BOOK PUBLISHING COMPANY

SMITH, CECIL-WOODHAM, THE GREAT HUNGER IN IRELAND, 1845-1899, 80 STRAND, LONDON, WC21R ORL, ENGLAND

WESTENDORF, P. THOMAS "I'LL TAKE YOU HOME AGAIN, KATHLEEN" NEW YORK 1875

Printed in the United States
By Bookmasters